A SHORT JOURNEY BY CAR

A Short Journey by Car

Liam Durcan

ESPLANADE
Books

THE FICTION SERIES AT VÉHICULE PRESS

Published with the generous assistance of The Canada Council for
the Arts, the Book Publishing Industry Development Program of
the Department of Canadian Heritage. and the Société de
développement des entreprises culturelles du Québec (SODEC).

Esplanade Books editor: Andrew Steinmetz
Cover design: David Drummond
Photo of author (page 203): Terence Byrnes
Set in Minion by Simon Garamond
Printed by AGMV-Marquis Inc.

LIBRARY AND ARCHIVES CANADA CATALOGUING IN PUBLICATION
Durcan, Liam
A short journey by car / Liam Durcan.
ISBN 1-55065-189-7
I. Title.
PS8607.U73S5 2004   C813'.6   C2004-904019-7

Published by Véhicule Press, Montréal, Québec, Canada
www.vehiculepress.com

Distribution in Canada: LitDistCo orders@lpg.ca
Distribution USA: Independent Publishers Group
www.ipgbook.com

Printed and bound in Canada.

To my family

Contents

ACKNOWLEDGEMENTS 8

A Short Journey by Car 11

Kick 24

Blood 28

Control 33

Lumière 53

Nightflight 62

The Gap 72

Cambodian Rock Song No. 4 79

dollyclocks 84

Nolan, an Exegesis 95

At First It Feels like Hunger 111

Generator 135

The Death of St. Clare 142

Recollection 146

The Blue Angel 155

American Standard 181

Acknowledgements

I'd like to thank the editors of the journals in which some of these stories appeared: Mark Jarman, Liz Phillips, Eric Bosse, Richard Cumyn, Robert Majzels, and Derek Webster. Matthrew Fox was particularly helpful for his edit of "Kick." For his friendship and fine editorial sense I would like to thank Andrew Steinmetz. I'm grateful to Jim and Maureen Durcan, Maria Higgins, and Anne McAuley. Finally, thank you Florence, Niall, and Julia, for your love and patience.

The stories appeared in different forms in the following journals: "A Short Journey by Car" (*Zoetrope All-Story Extra* and *Coming Attractions '03*), "Control" (*Grain*), "Blood" (*The Fiddlehead* and *Coming Attractions '03*), "Night Flight" (*Pottersfield Portfolio*), "dollyclock" (*The Paumanok Review*), "American Standard" (*The Fiddlehead* and *Coming Attractions '03*), "Lumière" (*The Antigonish Review*), "Cambodian Rock Song No. 4" (*Telling Stories: New English Fiction from Quebec*, Véhicule Press), "Nolan, an Exegesis" (*Maisonneuve*).

"Kick" won the 2003 CBC Montreal/ Quebec Writer's Federation Short Story competition.

Nothing is so difficult as not deceiving oneself.
  —Wittgenstein

A Short Journey by Car

A faith like a guillotine, as heavy, as light.
–Franz Kafka

Out of the darkness it arrives. Eyes open or closed, it comes without warning, perhaps because our eyes are never fully open. I listen and wait. Still, it comes as a surprise.

PHOTOGRAPH: MOSCOW, OCTOBER 1933

See him smile under that brush of a mustache; notice how the upper lip curls, exposing the crown of a bicuspid, its glistening tip like an inverted Matterhorn the depth of an iceberg in the Barents Sea. He shakes Kalinin's hand. In the official photo he is seen holding a pewter cup: Kalinin is gone. He is still smiling.

A STORY

I am pulled from my bed like any other man, my wife howling as they haul me away. How could she know that it was the start of something auspicious? After all, wonderful things rarely happen in the middle of the night, unannounced and with such haste. In my mind I review a list of the things that they could question about me, affiliations and memberships, what and whom I knew. We all live under the same fear, its presence like an atmospheric condition, a cold front that stalls above us and under which we shiver and curse.

Two men hustle me out of my apartment building, bundling

me down the stairs at such a rate our footsteps become a continuous clatter to which Mrs. Yusteva opens her door. She looks at me: bathrobe undone, hemorrhaging sweat from a stupefied face, a crazed peasant monk, and has not even the time to register a certain glee before she sees the men in their greatcoats and slams the door. We are outside for a moment in the paroxysmal cold and then in a car that is already moving, engine howling like a hungry wolf. I do not know where we are going but suspect these will be the last people I see and, reflexively, I ask nothing of them.

I believe we are headed to the outskirts of Moscow, to a linden grove in the pale light of morning, likely my last, when they suddenly turn north on Tormolev Street and stop at the foot of the building where I have my office. I am extracted with great force and expertise by two men who guide me now to the door of the building through which I pass like a spirit into the next world. I am transported to the landing of the fourth floor where I can see that the lights to my office are on and a contingent of officials awaits. I am shown to my examining room. Is this a dream now, not of linden woods but of a death made more terrible by its familiarity? May I now expect to see the spectral face of my father— a bottle held to his lips even in the next world—or experience the terror of sliding toward a precipice? An NKVD senior official—I know because he wears a hat and looks to be the one most enjoying the exhortations of the others—extends a hand toward my stool as if he were waiting for me all night, all my life. The patient is reclining in the chair, his mouth open, a big toe-sized thumb retracting his cheek, trying to lift the pain away.

COMRADE LEADER

Comrade Leader reclines semi-prone in my dental chair. I think it is Stalin. It looks like him. I have only ever seen photographs and in these he is always standing, but the NKVD breathing their threat and my heart sounding out against my ribs tell me it can be no one other than the Comrade Leader.

Dshugashvili. Everyone knows the eyes, but from a distance: among the generals, exhorting the worker, with the schoolchildren holding sheaves of wheat. For me the eyes offer no colour in particular, even at my proximity; the pupils are fully dilated, gobbling all the iris's pigment and now reflecting me, embossed in perspiration, gently running my two fingers over the surface of the gum around the offending tooth, *maxillary left "2" -3, class III cavity.* He winces and everyone reaches for their side-arms. I withdraw my fingers and for a moment think of a deserted linden grove.

"Calm, calm," the senior official says, to which my patient nods and the room exhales.

"It is not an abscess," I say, the first words I have uttered since I said goodnight to Anya six hours befor. "It would require some work, but the tooth could be saved."

My patient and the senior official look at each other and nod. The senior official clears the room and brings me closer with a motion of his gloved hand.

"There is the matter of the anaesthetic."

"Yes. I will use nitrous oxide."

"No."

I turn back to my patient, his eyes squinting in pain and fatigue, a mouth that could snap on my hands. I explain the procedure to him: remove a margin around the cavity, replace with an amalgam. He understands. He bobs his head. I touch the base of the tooth and the muscles of his mouth tense, his fists clench. I pull back and look at him.

"Your overall state of dental health is excellent, Comrade Leader."

He stares at me and I can smell wet cement floor, a room in the basement of Nikevsky Police Station, a drain at the center of that floor that I have heard has seen everything pass. He closes his mouth, licks those lips and asks me what nitrous oxide is, causing the senior official to cock his head in alarm. That is how they found me, I now understand, having used the nitrous on Semenov, a careerist party boss who cackled like an idiot even before the gas took effect, who was profuse in his thanks for my efforts at removing the remnants of a volcanically erupted molar, and was now, apparently, my enthusiastic supporter, my patron.

"An anaesthetic," I reply. "Something that will decrease the pain of the procedure."

"Isn't that dependent on the skill of the dentist?" he asks me. The senior official, head visible in my mirror, now tilts his head back ever so slightly, not suppressing his smile: a cracked incisor is visible, the work of a father's hand or the tools of one of my colleagues, either wielded in infamy.

"Comrade Leader, let me use the tools at my disposal to help you. Without the anaesthesia the procedure will be painful, try as I may. I do not want to cause unnecessary pain."

I show him my hands, extricated from the mouth of the tiger. He waves the senior official away; a door opens, the man leaves and from the face of the earth he drops: hat, tooth, man.

"Go ahead," he says, a smile curling his lips that must pain even him. "You'll likely need less gas for me than for Semenov."

ANYA
Her smile, modest and alluring as it is, is made more beautiful by the simple fact that I cannot remember it as ever needing to show me a single tooth.

MORNING
I am deposited at the door of our apartment. Mrs. Yusteva's door remains steadfastly closed. Anya has been crying, thinking that I will never return, cursing whoever may have provoked this: an aggrieved patient, Mrs. Yusteva, or her brother's writer friends who compose their rubbish and speak with indiscretion after drinking too much. She sobs into me, arms surrounding and thumping the cause of her livid morning.

LANGA, SECOND MAN ON THE MOUNTAIN, MAY 1936

In the annals of dental anesthesia, which are modes of political discourse like anything else, it is registered that an American, one Harry Langa, was the first to use nitrous oxide as anesthesia for a dental procedure. While an abscessed banker or perhaps a weeping press baron in need of dental relief may have allowed Dr. Langa's claim on posterity, what can be said with certainty is that he was not the first. What cannot be said, for reasons that should be evident, is that I was.

YURI

My partner Yuri, once he sees the disarray in which the office has been left and on whose behalf, wants to know what it felt like. What did it feel like? *I concentrated on my work; it felt like work.* He attempts to smile but has not been feeling well; he is dyspeptic and like me has been passed over for promotion at the university so many times that he does not smile as much as hold his lips in an expression that lies beyond indifference but short of contempt. For the rest of the day he works in silence as if the midnight consultation were a betrayal, as if they should have called on him. He eyes the bottles of nitrous that sit in the corner of my room and makes an effort to show me he has unrelated business in my office. He speaks idly, pretending to search for something in a cabinet.

> "Tell me about his teeth."
> "A typical mouth."
> "Is he to be your patient?"
> "I do not think so. I have not heard."
> "I can imagine his breath."
> I allow a modest laugh, "Straight from the devil's arse."

PHOTOGRAPH: SIBERIA, APRIL 1915

A man who is happy in exile. It is three years since he has joined the Central Committee and now he indulges himself in a small martyrdom. Dressed in black, a holdover from seminary days, he is seen smiling engagingly. He holds a cigarette in his left hand which is folded over his right. A space is visible between his front teeth. In later years he is more self-conscious, remembering to keep his mouth closed unless the situation absolutely calls for a smile.

Night Call

It is now a routine. In the midst of the trials they call again, still I do not merit a warning prior to the knock on the door—which has become our new national anthem, Anya's brother says. I tell Anya not to move, that I am certain that everything will be fine and so she does not stir from our bed. She is upset with me for tending to him, for having to tend to him. She whispers that he is a monster and that this is intolerable, to which I can say nothing. A new senior official this time, ushering me into and out of the car and then up to the office. I pray it is a different tooth. The NKVD henchmen clotted around the office are ashen-faced; he must have been roaring people into the next world. *Do you understand, dentist, that the leader must speak to the assembly this week?* I have no idea of his schedule but say that I understand, trying to steal a look at his open mouth, to see if it is the same tooth. I almost cry with relief when I see the abscess under a different lower molar, the gum glowing like a furnace. The senior official looms, sniffing for the gas, knowing the mistake his predecessor made. I tell myself that I will help Comrade Leader because a man in pain cannot take pity, a man in pain cannot use his wisdom to do justice, and so I set to work on draining the abscess. He looks at me and groans for the gas.

In the morning I return home to find Anya reading in the bedroom. She asks me if I know what is going on, how people from the historical society, professors from the university, are going missing. I do not know what she means by this, but I ask her what she would have me do. Would she have me refuse him? Provoke him to a higher madness? I am a dentist and can only do what I have been trained to do.

Photograph: Moscow, December, 1929

A glorious celebration of the fiftieth birthday in the Kremlin, December 21st, 1929, with party members Ordzhonikidze, Voroshilov, Kuibyshev, Kalinin, Kaganovich, and Kirov. All surround and congratulate, eyes trained toward the centre. Each face is a visage of forced gaiety, and not only because we are seeing things retrospectively; these men are smart enough to know their futures. A subdued smile, a congenial host, the Comrade Leader. They can almost sense the pain brewing in his jaw.

Results

It is months before I can speak to Anya with pride, and by that time it is in *White Tass* and *Pravda*, and on every lip in Moscow: he has shown pity. In the midst of a particularly difficult procedure (*full gold crown "2" 7-système internationale*), during which the gas was used liberally, but judiciously, I spoke to him about the situation of Titov, a man Anya knew and who earned the label of saboteur when he responded to Yaroslavsky's challenge to the Writer's Congress by tearing up his membership card in full view of the gathered assembly. Titov had become the subject of every second rumour in Moscow that summer: his behaviour at the congress, a collection of nonsensical poems published by an underground press, and accusations of unwholesome fornication, that last one tainting our family through the implication of Anya's brother. Comrade Leader smiled at the moment I exposed the base of his affected tooth and I knew that such intercessions, posed first to me by Anya, could be broached. I knew him well enough: I was after all his dentist, and to me he was as much a mouth full of individual problems as he was the Comrade Leader, and perhaps I was girded by whatever residual gas that had seeped into the room and found its way to my lungs. *Comrade Leader*, I said, *pity is a virtue of strong men*, to which he seemed to smile and acknowledged me with a fatherly, sagacious elevation of his brow. *Titov is a poet and not a good one at that. That much is agreed on, but he is not worthy of your displeasure.* He continued to nod, great brown moons of his eyes waning. *He will be forgotten, unless he is the object of your displeasure.* Comrade Leader looked out over the city and studied the cold blue light that broke on it. Silence. I read about it like everyone else. Like Langa, no one knows what I have done. The connection between saving Comrade Leader from inordinate pain and mercy shown to a poet will remain a mystery to all but her. Anya smiles and kisses me before she goes to her bed. The papers are folded and placed on the table, as I usually like to have them when I return home.

THE COLLEGE

We all have our Siberias, I tell him. He has become paradoxically maudlin, as he often does when he takes the gas, ruminating on his experiences in exile. The enamel has worn from his teeth with the grinding and all his pains are amplified. He asks me what my Siberia is and I tell him it is the dental college, my lack of success in getting a university appointment because I am seen as a dilettante, a huckster with a gas mask. He sits up and grabs my wrists in his hands, telling me that I am more than a dentist, that I am a compassionate healer and possess a scientific mind. His brows arch and his eyes, dark coals now with their inner fire visible, threaten to burst from their sockets. He tells me that my work exemplifies socialism: the conversion from a dream of a better future for humanity into a science. I should not worry, he says, letting his lids droop over his now-tearing eyes. I should not worry.

MARRIAGE

I meet Anya when she is twenty and still living with her father, a physician who specializes in diseases of the inner ear. He is a contemporary of Chekhov, a man for whom the doctor expresses such effusive admiration that the mere mention of the name induces vertigo in me. I think of fathers when I speak with him, of what sort of illness it is to be a father, to impose oneself on one's family like an affliction. Anya's father does not drink or bully, unlike the father I buried without a tear to help moisten the dirt. This man is a mild tickle in the throat, a transient dizziness. During our courtship I am often left alone with Dr. Rostropov in the parlour, discussing the importance of gooseberries, whose taste I do not enjoy, or the maladies of balance to which Muscovites are prone. The pall of these conversations is broken by the arrival of Anya. Arrival, it is such a modest word; she arrives as spring does, quietly infusing warmth and hope, inducing tender feelings in me that I have never known. Anya is a beauty and has eyes so expressive that I feel my dreams speaking out to me when I dare to look at them. We speak of music, which we both enjoy, and snow, to which we are both indifferent. We gain an understanding of the other's limits and aspirations. After our courtship she accepts my offer of marriage and we begin our lives together in Moscow.

She never wavers in her support of me; from my failure to have an appointment at the university to our inability to have a family. After her father dies we take in her brother Anton, who stays with us for three years. She remains steadfast.

PROMOTION
An appointment as lecturer in the newly established department of dental anesthesia. I prepare notes for my course and lecture to rows of bobbing heads. My hand shakes, I am told, when I speak and so I place it in my pocket, which I imagine lends me an avuncular air. Any questions? None. Well then, you will be examined on this later. I am appalled by the perfunctory approach of my colleagues, who seem willing not just to authorize but endorse slapping the mask on the face of the patient until there is no response, not understanding that the goal is to achieve a sense of well-being in the patient, not unconsciousness. I am viewed with some skepticism in my department, but, as I say, so as not to err in policy, one must be a revolutionary, not a reformer. Yuri handles the bulk of work at the office, picking up where I have left off,

tending to Politburo wives, occasionally their husbands, and the aching jaws of NKVD men, none of which he sees fit to thank me for.

A promotion follows months later; vacancies have arisen, and now heads nod in our department meetings when I speak. Another year and I am an associate professor, bringing the department into the twentieth century, an era when our profession will not be one of punition but of preservation and restoration. Surveillance of dental disease, I tell my colleagues as I have told Comrade Leader, is the key. Dentistry is like the state, I almost say to him at the end of a composite restoration *mandibular right "4" 6, extraction mandibular right "4" 7—système internationale*, and requires a political awareness of small things, a meticulous observation of detail.

My ascent has not gone unnoticed by my colleagues. I am studied; a new tooth in the mouth, probed for imperfections and held in some wonder. *You are in full flight, Yevgeny Mikailovich*, my chairman says, eyeing me cautiously, *watch the sun*.

Occlusal Surface of the First Molar
In contrast to the pre-molars, the cusps become more prominent, and by the nature of these surfaces and their physical characteristics it can be seen why most of the grinding of mastication takes place here. The occlusal surface has four cusps—distolingual, distobuccal, mesiolingual, and mesiobuccal. The fifth cusp, the cusp of Carabelli, can be seen when the tooth is viewed occlusally, but does not form part of the occlusal surface.

The Siege
The Comrade Leader returns to me with his aching jaws, as though he has been the one chewing on rats in Leningrad. Despite the pain, he wears his other worries lightly. He falls asleep during the procedure, dreaming of what I do not know. I turn the valve of the nitrous tank to the right, a quarter turn, enough to have the

Comrade Leader awaken as I continue working. It feels as though the room is filling with cold water. A man must gird himself.

FATHER, A DIALECTIC

A man who possessed property but not the consciousness of the contradictions that it engendered. A man who could not make sense of the world as it changed, and who tried to comprehend it through systematic brutality directed at his family. A man invoking the past that was a lie, seeking solace in icons and the humiliation of others under his hand. A man for whom rage and powerlessness found their true home. A saboteur and progenitor. An enemy, a man, a bourgeois villain. My father.

INTERVENTION

Under my gaze—will the books ever know of it? There will be stories of those who derailed trains, or fired the next first-shot and whose noisy subterfuge was heroic only in its lack of humility. What of the man who dismantles the guillotine? What of me, beseeching him as the gas flows and I undo all that his sloth and vanity have done to those smooth surfaces, what of me, scaling and probing to reduce the chance that he will pass on all the pain that he has ever had?

His mouth and its contents of worn boulders are no longer a mouth but the source from which all emanates. His mouth is created and recreated with my hands, under my will. His mouth opens and it is no longer a naturalist's excursion; something has changed when I gaze in.

PHOTOGRAPH: YALTA, FEBRUARY 1945

Roosevelt, for a rich man, has terrible oral hygiene. Gingivitis by his early thirties has endowed him with periodontal problems that plague him in later years. He smiles, seated beside the other two, yellow roots gleaming at the world. It is a travesty that no one attends to this. One half-expects him to dislodge a molar with his next hacking catarrh. It is clear to the others that he is not long for this world. It is enough to say that Churchill has false teeth that rattle.

Apogee

Less than two months after I am announced head of the department of the university's school of dental anaesthesia, in a grand but sombre ceremony that Comrade Leader cannot attend but at which I am honoured by the unanimous attendance of my department, Anya tells me that she is ill. I look at her, as I do every morning but now it is as though I have not seen her at all. Her eyes, her face. She recedes, a day falling into night, before my eyes. Another fifty-three days.

As I am cleaning out Anya's belongings I come across her correspondence. I leaf through the letters, looking for some sign not just of her but of something else, something I cannot admit at the time but for which I long; a sonnet to her, impossibly from Titov or letters from another useless novelist declaring his love for her, something profane, proof of acts committed, a legion of sentiment. There are only letters from her sister whose contents speak to matters of limited domestic interest.

A Short Journey by Car

As any other night goes, so this one does. Out of the darkness it arrives. New faces at the door and then more at the wheel of the car, some of them NKVD I have seen loitering in Yuri's office. A moon of a scleral blue sits in the western sky. I am not shocked when we pass Tormolev Street because I am this moon, its reflections and slow course around the world in daylight and darkness. The NKVD men perspire but I do not, perhaps because it is I who watch them. No explanation is offered when the car stops next to a field and the door opens. The youngest of them takes me by the arm in a way that befits the chairman of a department and leads me across the stubble and cracked earth, raising dust in the moonlight. There are no linden trees, nothing except the limits of vision and now I am alone facing them under this endless, radiant sky. They are all young, most not yet used to this and they will not sleep well regardless of what I do, but I smile. Their right arms rise in unison, as though offering me assistance. I wait for something to break this night, another burst of light, a morning star.

Kick

I was seven years old when I suddenly realized that very young babies were being flung into the local swimming pool. This was quickly followed by the shock that my own baby sister—freshly pink and implacable—was one of those being tossed. Of course, all this was done under the fretful gaze of my mother who, like the other mothers, would stand in the waist-deep water while the fathers stooped at poolside and gently dropped their infant children. After the hush there would be a grand, syncopated splash and then the mad scramble of baby retrieval in the foam.

My girlfriends and I, shapeless bodies hidden under our bikinis, watched this in silence from the springboards at the other end of the pool, stupefied. We had grown up with the conviction—burned into consciousness by our parents—that water, although great fun, presented countless enticements to death. And so we lived with ironclad parental injunctions, veritable commandments of swim-ming: the thirty-minute post-lunch wait, the no-spitting-water rule, the zero tolerance policy on horseplay. We had water wings and flutter boards clamped to us and were subjected to swimming lessons so unremitting and arduous that it should have alerted child welfare authorities. Whenever fatigue or faltering technique caused us to begin to sink, our swim coaches would exhort us with the universal command intended to forestall drowning: *kick*, they screamed. We kicked a lot. So the change in our parents' attitudes—almost more than the act of throwing babies into the pool—caught us completely by surprise; I stood on the springboard, gape-mouthed. Anything was possible.

Soon after that I remember seeing this sort of activity shown repeatedly on television. Footage from underwater cameras captured the crystalline splash of countless babies like my sister. The infants were always shown paddling through clear blue water, looking infinitely pleased and confident, like astronauts on a spacewalk. This was the new way to learn to swim. Humans were natural swimmers, it was argued; lessons and graphic warnings only generated unnecessary fear, estranging us from our natural, amphibian tendencies. And so the flinging began.

My mother now downplays her participation in the baby-flinging method of swim training that gripped the nation in those days, although when it's mentioned, like now when I bring it up in the spirit of communal nostalgia, she defends the action, or more precisely, the motivation behind it.

"It made your sister a great swimmer," she says.

Janet lifts her head enough that we can all register the basset-hound arch of her eyebrow.

"Well, you *are*," she continues, always retaining the right to be offended by the incredulity of her daughters.

My mother gets up to clear away the emptied tea cups and the plate with two remaining shortbread cookies, clearly performing the act with more vigour than is necessary. An undisguised clattering in the sink, the audible snap of a dish towel.

"You *had* to mention it," Janet drones, not looking up from the curling pieces of paper in front of her.

I close my eyes. From outside my kitchen window the reports of crickets rise, almost drowned out by the adenoidal hiss of the baby monitor. The cupboard door claps closed in punctuation. A breeze sifts through the rooms on the first floor, gently eddying doors on their hinges. I imagine the air pouring upstairs like an ocean current, brushing my sleeping son's hand, rippling under the crib that holds my daughter. Tonight the whole house feels like a giant animal taking short skimming breaths. My sister shifts to get comfortable under her growing stomach. She exhales after this maneuvre, the effort almost sufficient to create a sigh. My mother, hurt feelings forgotten, returns to the table. When I open my eyes, they're sitting there just as I've imagined, which shocks and delights me.

My sister stares intently at the image in front of her, disengaging only to shuffle the papers and view the next. A pointillist work in black and white clusters that form a line or a swirl that from a distance could represent the gathering winds of a hurricane. But on the paper that has her name on its corner she swears that she can make out the curve of a human forehead, tracing it with her forefinger. In another, a heart is caught between its humming-bird beats. My favourite is one where out of complete visual chaos a perfect gloved hand of delicate bone emerges, as though pressed up against a pane of glass.

"They don't tell you the sex anymore, do they?" I say.

"Lawsuits," Janet replies. "People paint the baby's room pink, buy dresses and choose girls' names, all based on the ultrasound and…whoops."

"Still, that's a lovely surprise," my mother says, "a little penis." She pauses after saying 'penis', as though luxuriating in the reticent thrill. Grandchildren have made it safe for her to say the word in company.

When I was pregnant with my first I was as excited and curious as anyone but those books designed to tell you what to expect during pregnancy seemed vague or focused on issues like properly decorating the baby's room; so instead I bought an embryology textbook from the university bookstore and read about what was happening inside me. The diagrams showed how the cells moved in an orderly way to form a plate that pinched and folded into a tube. In this way a brain was assembled, its surface corrugating, connections made that would eventually be another universe. Within weeks a shrimp-shaped mass had budded limbs and taken on a human form, cells streaming in every direction, bringing a body into existence. It was as though I could hear the activity

humming inside me. Janet's husband Bob, who's an anaesthesi-
ologist, once found me reading the book and hovered silently over
my shoulder. He said nothing but I knew what he was thinking.
He was right I suppose; it did keep me awake nights, thinking about
the complexity of the whole thing, the journeys that had to be
completed. All those contingencies. When my son was born, fan-
tastically normal, I put the book away. For my second it stayed on
the shelf.

The monitor crackles, relaying the stirrings of my daughter
down to us. We look at each other, all of us silent for a moment,
waiting for her voice to call out for me, but nothing comes. Janet
has finished studying the last of her ultrasound pictures. It shows
the clearest image of her unborn child floating in a sea of deepest,
amniotic black. She's happy, of course, but she also has that other
look, an extra furrow that I've worn and that I'm certain my mother
knows as well. For anyone looking in at us through the window of
this suburban house I suppose we three must appear to be a picture
of contentedness, even self-satisfaction. But my sister's face shows
more than that. She hears the hum. Yes, it's different here at the
table, more complicated. I just sit beside her, thinking of what I
can say to help, but no words seem to do. Besides, in a moment a
kick will come without anyone's urging.

Blood

I didn't know you could die from a bleeding nose.

He is shouting at me, face deep in a sodden towel. His voice is muffled and faintly gurgling but there is a resonance that I could never mistake. He tells me to go through the red light—he can sense me stopping and will not have it. *Go, go,* he bellows from his towel. I look up over the dashboard to get a better view of the intersection and he is at it again, *for Christ's sake go,* he says, the last word warbled in blood. I step on it and hear a horn blast as I pass through the intersection. For the first time I feel the power in the car, the intent in the roar beneath the floorboard and wait for the sound of a siren that doesn't come.

He took blood thinners. A pill every day depending on how thick his blood was. The hospital would leave a message to take a half a pill more or less, depending on the blood test. His blood was never just right; the dose was always changing. I remember as a kid trying to figure out what that meant—having blood that was either too thick or thin. They would ask on the phone if he had a beer or ate a lot of green vegetables. Oh yeah, a great one for salads, he is.

We pass the elevated railway crossing and he groans into his towel as the road drives us up with a sick-joke promise of becoming airborne, but the Galaxie 500 is a flightless bird and it only shudders over the tracks, plumage of rust disintegrating with each mile and moment. If it could bleed it would. He is quieter now.

It must be too thin. Mike took the message, scribbled it down on the pad and then slapped it on the fridge. I remembered how the note paper, with the thin line of adhesive along the top, looked like a little yellow awning flapping into the room. But I didn't read what Mike wrote on the paper and I doubted the old man had either. The note was still there when we left, broad and pug-nosed smack in the middle of the great avocado-green face of the fridge.

Again with the horn, but I have picked up too much speed to consider hitting the brakes going through the yield. I can sense the old man almost smile through the bloody towel. I reach under the seat to find the handle that allows me to pull myself forward, clawing the dark, scattering the beer cans and paper refuse before catching it. I yank the latch and hump the seat forward but the manoeuvre doesn't work; I am left peering over the dash as I perch on the seat's edge.

Now the wind funnels through the car as I push it past sixty down Archibald Street, past the bungalows that dapple and fade out of my peripheral vision, past the oncoming shapes of the packing houses whose dimensions elongate and lean in, features and colour fading into monoliths. *Take the left, take the left*, he says, he knows where we are. He knows perfectly well.

I am still counting the times that I have been in the driver's seat. The perforations in my learner's permit are not yet completely creased, my signature is still fresh under the box checked off to indicate my willingness to cede my organs, my first solemn duty. I have a routine of adjusting the instruments around me, something that Mike mocks by way of shouting—*rear flap! …rear flap operational*—but it is a routine: side- and rear-view mirrors, seat, and finally the radio. It calms me before the ignition catches, a ritual as real as the placement of a dashboard virgin or the scrotal tumble of fuzzy dice, and not half as distracting. Today I had no chance to go through the rites. I found him a towel and wiped off my hands before grabbing the keys from the kitchen table and that was it. I am paying the price now, having to hike the seat up on the fly, jerking my feet forward and having one slip off the accelerator, producing a chrissake from the old man. Side-view, rear-view, seat.

I glance at the mirrors. I am triangulated by the time we are at Marion Street and I scream into a left turn, the one light I make—the one I *have* to make—and I want him to say something or at least let on that he thinks that I have made the turn through traffic, against the light. I pull the car out of the wake of a bus, cutting in front of a Nissan, and feel a wobble in the handling accompanied by his groan. I look over to see his hands compressing the towel against his head, pale half-moons of his nails against the darkening sky. *Oh*, he says.

He had a bad heart. It was scarred by rheumatic fever. *Licks the joints but bites the heart*, I heard someone say once, but it wasn't him because he didn't talk about such things. Achilles heel, I remember thinking one time after he slapped me. If you could find the heart you knew it would be bad: a bag of evil humour. Rheumatic fever left him a valve that disconsolately flapped like the note on the refrigerator. His heart skipped beats and was prone to throwing off clots, as if to spite the other parts of his body for harbouring such a heart. He refused to have a mechanical valve put in, made a fuss about it too, right there in the clinic, in front of all those doctors and nurses and other patients, probably for the benefit of his boys. Mike and I just sat there, shrinking under the twin fists of fear and shame. Blood thinners were the only compromise he would make.

Blood is pounding in my neck and chest and now everything seems magnified. On my left we pass a park, violently protesting its colours, throbbing green now out of the depths where the river cleaves it. It isn't illegal; he's right there, that's what a learner's permit is. Everybody's got to learn. *What?* he says because I have said this out loud. I feel the car roar beneath me, underneath the rigours of its frame, sensing the cylinders and valves and the controlled explosion at the core of it all.

Mike left the night before and had not come back this morning. I checked his room every hour during the night but the bed stayed empty. The house was quiet for the first time in weeks but I wanted him to come back. You're like the old man, he said, you need voices around the place. Mike didn't need voices, or if he did it wasn't the old man's: raised, directed, tinged with mundane profanity. Even before the old man and I sat down for breakfast and he started rattling on about the faggot, before I had even gone into his room to find the drawers of the dresser half-closed in a parting salute, I had the feeling that he wasn't coming back.

The tires whine through the turn that takes us onto Goulet and he has pretty much stopped groaning. I ask him how he's doing and he nods his head. The hair on the back of his head tapers down to a point on the nape of his neck, matted and dewed with sweat. It was easy to understand why he didn't talk about his heart, why he refused the operation and took prescriptions as suggestions: he is a man who works with his hands, who defines himself physically. On a refinery tower, at that height, balancing on a platform in the toxic plumes, a man's scars should come with an explanation more exotic, more heroic than just the best interests of his family.

And he worked, that much you had to give to him. He was a horse or a mule or whatever animal is best made to suffer incremental indignities in the guise of labour and not be aware of any of it because it came with a paycheck. That was what Mike said. He wouldn't have said that to the old man. He knew the old man's limits, he seemed to be testing them every day in a debate conducted at high volume—until something was said last night, and now he was gone. The bed wasn't touched.

The road descends once I pass Desmeurons Street and I am alone now; no learner's permit or stricken father or brother gone except for the map of himself on the bed sheets. I am alone with the sound of a glass breaking on the ground and with his voice rising. What will I say to the doctor? They will want to know how this happened. A mechanism of injury, a term remembered from trips to the emergency room when Mike or I would look the nurse in the eye and tell stories of errant doors—*it swung in, I thought it would swing out*—or graceless athletics exploits. I am alone with my explanation: he is on blood thinners, this happens, he drinks, my fist swung into his face like a door from a darkened recess. He pushed me and I felt threatened.

Go, go, he says and I wonder what he means. With his head wrapped and tottering I wonder what he has ever meant. He says go; it means nothing more. I am flying, catching all the lights, the illuminated cross of the hospital now in view and looming. It is absolutely quiet, as though the engines have cut and we are now drifting, finding our place without effort, everything is silent and effortless, falling in love or asleep, falling apart.

That lasts for a moment. The car is under my control, it is my movements mirrored in metal and rubber. Nothing is effortless. I staggered him with my right hand and before the torrent started I saw the look in his eyes. Everything had changed.

Straight ahead lies the Norwood Bridge that leads into the city centre, a left turn would take me out of the city completely, to limitless highway and space but I flip the indicator on to signal the right turn for the hospital. The sky framing the hospital is split by a mantle of cloud the colour of burnished metal and it is this image, this lack of shape and colour that leaves me feeling lonely, only it's not that but something that feels like loneliness. I don't know what it is but it has an authenticity I will remember: the dishwater light, the ache of my right hand, the taste in my mouth. He throws open the door and gets to the emergency room entrance. I hope he will ask me to come in with him, to have my hand looked at, but no. I reach out and turn the radio on. I will go in later, to give the doctors his particulars and watch them stanch the bleeding. I will see his pallor and the harried action around him as his life is contemplated. But now all I do is sit and let the radio drown everything out for no reason other than there are words in my head and a voice that is rising; my words, my voice, and there is nothing so ugly as a man coming into his own.

Control

HYPNOTICA
It all started to change when something unusual fell out of Gerald's ear. He recognized the signs only after the object had been delivered: an alteration in his hearing followed by a vague hiccupping in the tubes—as though final preparations for landing were being made—and then finally, the jiggle. By the time he found a Q-tip it was no longer needed: a peanut-sized object had already dislodged itself and had come to rest on the little cartilage shelf of his ear lobe.

In his hand the object looked like a bug or a piece of rock the colour of a beer bottle. A translucent hair emerged from its underside like a flagellum. He was appalled and fascinated and pushed it around with the Q-tip. Gerald was surprised at now being able to hear more clearly and he smiled, overcome by a momentary sense of well-being. He wanted to tell someone but decided against it, and instead, after carefully wrapping the object in a Kleenex, dropped it into the toilet where it cycloned down another, far darker hole.

Gerald could not sleep that night. At first he thought it was his restored hearing, for the apartment murmured and groaned around him, but he soon realized that the source of his restlessness was speculation about what other surprises lurked inside him. He was young, he repeated to himself as he stared at the ceiling, he had years ahead of him, and he tried to reassure himself that thoughts of his deterioration—a faint rattling in his lungs, an embolus that no doubt circulated through him like a suicide bomber's laden truck—were nothing more than paranoia. Unconvinced, he lay awake in anticipation of the tug of a gallstone or an aneurysm's merciless boot-kick to his head, but only morning came. Eventually he got up and turned on the television.

It was the arrival of mail that awoke him from the couch. For a moment he was disoriented and was relieved to see letters pouring through the slot. He looked at the clock. It was past eleven. He thought about calling in to work to let them know that he couldn't make it, but at this hour Mr. Margolese would regard his call as a provocation. And then a confluence of circumstances occurred: as he sat on the sofa, eyeing the final notice for an unpaid bill, plagued with thoughts of bodily dissolution and inevitable confrontations with his boss, he saw a familiar television advertisement looking for participants in drug studies. *Eureka*. The ad scrolled out in its predictable way but it revealed something new to him. Happy faces of subjects beamed out from the Naugahyde depths of their La-Z-Boy recliners. A nurse distributed Dixie cups that they cheerfully emptied. All very clean, first class stuff. They all appeared pleased and relaxed, as if aboard a charter flight to someplace warmer. *You will be remunerated, you will be screened.*

Gerald put down the mail. He repeated the Institute's telephone number out loud until he got to the phone. The melody of the touch-toned numbers soothed him, and made the wait for a voice at the other end more tolerable. A few minutes later he put down the receiver. An appointment for an interview, that's what he got.

The Institute's headquarters was a facility of glass and concrete laid out campus-style on the edges of the city. Beyond the great glass doors that slid open and then closed in opposition like perfect tectonic plates, he entered a peaceful kingdom of mahogany inlays and high quality furniture: feng shui of the gods. A wonderful smell surrounded him; the essence of meadow or mountaintop had been captured and circulated through the vaulted foyer. Gerald took a lungful of the cool air and could almost sense a therapeutic effect. He was greeted by a woman whose smile seemed entirely sincere and voluntary, and was directed to the evaluation officer.

The Briquet Institute was a contract research organization that ran phase one studies, which, it was explained to him before the film was screened and as the questionnaires were handed out, were the crucial studies to prove medications weren't lethal. This was the necessary step before the FDA-scrutinized, double-blinded-roll-of-the-dice phase two and three studies designed to demonstrate their benefit. Once the animal work was done (it all sounded wonderfully agrarian, so cautious and evolutionary), they could start dose escalations of healthies. That was what he hoped he was, a *healthy*—or that was what they were about to determine, God bless them.

A screen was lowered and the room darkened.

Arthritis, congestive heart failure, dementia—the film's narrator intoned as the camera swooped over the countryside toward the facility— *illness is the last obstacle to happiness.* A world wanting to be healthy demanded progress and the Briquet Institute, with its dedicated research faculty and associates, was on that leading edge of *healing.* A man Gerald's age but several inches taller passed out the questionnaires and, stopping in front of Gerald, addressed the group with seminarian earnestness.

"Everyone be honest now, we have projects tailored to just about everyone, but we need you to be honest with us."

Gerald looked around and saw every head in the room bent in attention over their packages. Pages began to turn and he imagined he could hear the hum of mental effort.

EXCITANTIA
"Money. Straight up, for me, it's the cash."

Gerald awoke from a light sleep to hear the young man in the next reclining chair expounding on his reasons for choosing the Institute. Chuck was quite likely still a teenager and given his state of ceaseless motion—a series of tics and finger drummings, gang hand-signs and a right foot that wriggled like a fish on a line— Gerald guessed he had only recently let his Ritalin prescription lapse. While Chuck rattled away to the nurses who smiled and took blood pressures and filled vacuum tubes of blood, Gerald closed his eyes for a moment more, only to be roused as the tourniquet was being loosened from his arm. He was having difficulty staying awake. The battery of multiple choice questions, repetitive and occasionally lurid, was exhausting. The questions were intensely personal, but he felt more insulted by their perfunctory tone. It was as like being interrogated by a border guard who happened to be a former girlfriend.

– Mean income.
– Birth order.
– Musical preferences—circle one (AOR/ ROCK/ C&W/ JAZZ/ BLUES/ CLASSICAL/ CLASSICS-OLDIES/ RAP/ HIP-HOP/ TRIP-HOP/ DANCE/ FACTORY/ TECHNO & TRANCE/ HOUSE/ HOUSE-GARAGE/ HEAVY METAL/ THRASH / DEATH).

Death? What was Death? He felt anxious at not having better genre awareness, especially after his ill-advised record club transactions, but he had to lift his hand.

The invigilators consulted: "Death Metal," he was told.

Fast food consumption. Bowel movements per week. He put down a number preceded by *approx.* to indicate an awareness short of checking the bowl or actually keeping a count.

This was followed by the personality inventory, which made the first questionnaire seem as psychologically invasive as a bus stop chat about el Niño. He felt ashamed by the end, as though he had nothing left to himself except that little clump of whatever had fallen out of his ear—and now even that was gone. Thank God they didn't know about that.

At the end of the second day, following a rigorous physical examination that left him breathless and sweaty, he and the half-dozen other associates were escorted to the debriefing room and told that they had graduated. They were healthies. An attractive woman with pulled-back hair who wore a lab coat—impossibly clean, laser pleated—told the group that they would soon be contacted by the Institute concerning the projects on offer. *We have your contact numbers*, she said, unveiling her send-off smile and folding her arms over the shield of her clipboard.

Gerald had lost track of the time and was surprised to see that the day was ending; the sun had slipped behind pink petrochemical clouds. There was a faint stink of heavy industry among the other odours of the world. Upon reaching the bottom step of the administration building, the group seemed set to disperse when they all stopped, looking at each other, uncertain if they were to remain strangers.

It was Chuck, of course, who suggested that they all go out for a celebratory drink, which stunned them for a moment, as they wondered if this was allowed of associates, not the fraternization as much as the pollution of the alcohol, second-hand smoke, and red dye number five.

"So is anybody up for happy hour at the Spoon?"

The two young Asian women in the group regarded Chuck warily. The younger of the two sisters, Jacqueline, swung a backpack over her shoulder and appeared ready to say no, but instead smiled and nodded avidly. Her sister Carolyn had no choice after that. The others, a guy with a prepubertal frame and a baseball hat and the old man in the hockey jacket who constantly stroked his beard, seemed amused at Chuck's efforts, and said that, yes, they would join too.

That left Gerald, who did not as a rule enjoy situations where he would be forced into making chit chat. He had to be publicly goaded by Chuck before he agreed to come along. There had been a time, Gerald reminded himself as they entered the bar and were assaulted by the unique despair that is a happy hour-in-progress, when he had been more resolute in his indifference, when he would have told Chuck to fuck off as he had so many ill-matched room-mates or telemarketers, but now, and maybe it was the fatigue or the effects of an anemia induced by the day's many phlebotomies, he resigned himself to talk of sports or the current popular outrage.

Under the big screen television they sat in a fellowship of embarrassed silence: Chuck, almost hyperventilating between the two young women, Ivan in the ballcap and Mr. Peterangelo who already had a beer in hand before the rest of them had settled at the table. By the time a tray of drinks arrived they had found common ground, telling each other how they had come to the Institute. Ivan had student loans that were mounting and Peterangelo spoke in vague terms about a second mortgage. Carolyn said that she and her sister were interested in research and wanted to help in any way they could. Hearing her graceless lie convinced Gerald to abandon his story about a sick relative whom he felt obliged to help, and instead he spoke of exorbitant veterinarian bills racked up by a beloved, theoretical Rottweiler. Jacqueline wanted to know what sort of problems the breed was prone to; they had all heard of horrific genetic disorders in dogs: disintegrating hips, tails that wouldn't wag, berserk Dalmatians who chewed their own legs off.

"He's going blind," Gerald said in a halting voice, surprising himself with every word of the new lie. He could almost imagine the dog sniffing out the dark world, with his master beside him, his faithful seeing-eye person.

"Oh shit, that's awful," Ivan said.

"I'm sorry," said Jacqueline, touching his arm.

They emptied their glasses and ate the free popcorn from baskets that sat every few feet along the bar. Jacqueline and Carolyn flushed with the first sip of their light beers. Gerald drank a soda water and bit into the lemon wedge that accompanied it. He could imagine Margolese ranting over accounts drifting to other companies because of his truancy, how the perennial threat of termination hung in the air. Gerald washed the sour taste out of his mouth with the last of his drink. On the television in the far corner of the bar, the huge pink melon of a sportscaster's head appeared in widescreen glory. He was a personality familiar to Gerald, an over-decibeled crank whose spray of saliva could be felt by his audience. The big head's lips moved but the volume on the television was turned down, and instead the bar was filled with piped-in music. Gerald was squinting at the moving lips, puckering and vitriolic, spattering in silence, when suddenly, the lips and the music seemed to be in sync for a moment. He turned back to what he hoped would be the less disturbing inanities of his tablemates. As he gave himself over to eavesdropping on their conversations, he was surprised that they began to intrigue him, gathered around the table in a camaraderie befitting off-duty test pilots, swagger and fear in their voices. He wondered if they were all like him, fearful of the coming disasters, the moment when their opportunities would quickly come to nothing. He was thirty years old and had done little with his life, and maybe that was why he had been sleepless, he thought, watching Chuck chat up a waitress after annoying Carolyn and Jacqueline. Since his four years at an innocuous university, he had belayed from job to job for almost a decade, and the only saving grace was that he had no friends with full, happy lives against which his would stand in even sharper contrast.

What did he have? An apartment filled with prefabricated furniture, a couch and television and the abyss between. What did he have other than the inaugural tingles of carpal tunnel syndrome when he cradled the remote? He could not remember the last time he'd gone out on a date. It wasn't as though he had been unhappy, but now he was aware of the draught horse's goofy, stupid smile that he imagined he wore. Where were the big ideas? Why had he been so untested? So asleep? It all seemed clear to Gerald now: death, although feared, had been the most interesting possibility. It had awakened him. His life was a death and that death a hell as surely as if Margolese himself were the devil digging the pitchfork into his ass and turning him on a spit. He would change his life. He ordered another soda water.

EUPHORICA

Within the week, Gerald received a couriered package that contained notice of his first tests and a small plastic case of medications, twenty-eight tablets that he was warned may leave a metallic taste in his mouth and cause him to urinate more often. Also in the package was the agreement stipulating the reimbursement (an impressive sum that made him re-check the zeros) that would be paid to him in a month's time, when the study was over and he had completed all the blood tests and had his bronchoscopy, a test to look inside the tubes of his lungs. He called the office to ask Margolese for a leave of absence, and when he got the old man on the phone something came over him and he resigned on the spot. After emptying his bladder, he went outside for a walk.

He saw the rest of the group at the Test Centre every day: Ivan was healing after a skin biopsy and Chuck staggered around in distress because of the low protein diet he was on—part of a study involving a fourth generation cephalosporin antibiotic. Jaqueline and Carolyn had become subjects of great interest because they were *mtp's*, monozygotic twin pairs—identical twins—and therefore a highly prized research resource.

"I was sure we were dizygotes," Carolyn said, unable to hide her disappointment.

"I guess it's better for us this way," replied Jacqueline, bemused at the thought as she scanned the results of the genetic testing that had sealed their fate. "It doubles payment, you see, for each of us."

"I feel dizygotic, though," her sister said, looking up through the atrium at a great blue circle of sky.

They settled into the routine of tests and each other's company, and other than Mr. Peterangelo's absence—there was a rumour of abnormal liver function tests that had disqualified him from a test of new anti-malarials—they grew to recognize themselves as a cohort, with a solidarity of purpose. Gerald took his pills, and for the first time in his memory he was happy and conscious of it. By the third night of the study he had begun having unusual experiences, side effects not mentioned in the package insert but which he nonetheless dutifully noted in the study log:

06/18   23.30 Unable to sleep. Awoke approximately 23.15—multiple jerking movements of legs. Headache noted—mild (3/10) Erection noted…Dreams—increased activity, altered content. ?Talking animals—in black and white…. Need to urinate.

06/19   00.00 Slept for twenty minutes, profound jerking of right arm, left leg, no headache (1/10). Markedly more pronounced erection coinciding with nightmare of falling. Nausea (3/10).

06/21   01.50 Nightmares—intense content, a dog on television bursts through the screen, am then underwater but can breathe. No headache. Erection—persistent (8/10). Incontinence of urine.

What he didn't note in the log book or tell the research co-ordinator, what he kept to himself like a sweet visitation, was the ecstasy. He rationalized that because they did not ask him to list it, he could remain silent with a clear conscience; and besides, what was happening, now night after night, billowing in its intensity, was not only new for him, but something that he doubted could be described. It stunned him, fully and completely; the wrenching pull from sleep, the prescient lull, the rush.

It wasn't as though he was inexperienced; in his college years he regularly doused his synapses with the most popular mind-altering substances of his generation. He had his war stories: seismic headaches, pangs of the stupid hunger that followed a turn at the bong, the cheery gulag of a rave. He had seen his share of friends disappear into their personal elevator shafts of addiction and took pains to avoid them as they twelve-stepped their way back into his life. He abandoned drugs not because of a grand moral dictum but because they bored him and gave him headaches. But this, this was clearly different: out-of-body experiences, the feeling of absolute freedom and overwhelming authenticity. His previous drug exposure had not been by any means encyclopedic; he had dodged the mushroom in university—at the time dismissing it as another low-yield con—but now he knew the dark secret of the jabbering psilocybenoids. This was pure experience.

Gerald dared not ask what was in the pills given to him by the Institute, but assumed that the bronchoscopy and samplings were largely a ruse and that it was the drug itself and the new good mood it induced that were the focus of the study, that the pills he swallowed nightly were some form of a psychotropic medication soon to be widely dispersed for a greater good. In his ample spare time between visits to the Institute to give stool and semen samples—not bad money for manual labour, Chuck prated— Gerald cruised the stacks at the university library for guides to hallucinogens, hungering for more information about what was happening inside him. He commandeered a study carol in the library. A wall of books formed on his table. He read about hallucinogens used in sacred rituals and Hoffman's work in the development of LSD. But it was beside a copy of Lewin's *Guide to Psychoactive Agents* that he finally struck gold in the form of a biography of Richard Evans Schultes.

Schultes was an ethnobotanist, *the* ethnobotanist, with thousands of plant species to his name and a reputation that combined scientific discovery, careful anthropologic observation, and mind-blowing drug parties with whatever indigenous people in whose forest he found himself trespassing. Gerald read on like the ink was oxygen.

June 1937—Schultes, then an undergraduate at Harvard, chooses to write about *Lophophora williamsii* (Cactaceace) —the peyote cactus—for his thesis, and is encouraged to travel to Oklahoma to have first-hand experience with the plant. He spends the summer with the Kiowa Indians, learning about their ceremonial rites, sampling the plant and seeing amazing colours, topping it off with a first-rate thesis and an invitation to the doctoral program.

October 1941—the doctoral thesis brings Schultes to Mexico in search of the sacred mushroom of the Aztecs. He travels alone, without a weapon and with minimal gear, using his skills as an observer to record, for the first time, the customs of the local tribes, and is eventually introduced to Teonanacatl (*Panaeolus campanulatus*). More lab work, munch, munch, and then the doctorate.

February 1942—after months cataloguing wild Hevea species, Schultes treks overland from Bogota to the tiny village of Porto Limón where he stays for weeks with the Ingano tribe, imbibing *yagé* (*Banisteriopsis caapi*), which the local healers, or *curanderos*, take to attain visions of what herb their sick patient needs. Schultes can barely tolerate the bitter taste of *yagé*, and notices most of the *curanderos* combine it with *chagropanga* (*Diplopterys cabrerana*) which splinters the dull violet visions of yagé with dazzling colour and light, and, perhaps more importantly, makes the whole concoction palatable. It takes years for neurochemists to explain the underlying chemistry of the *chagropanga*-chaser effect; what remains unknown is how it could have been discovered among the thousands of other active agents in the forest depths.

It would be wrong of course, Gerald knew, to think of Schultes as just some trippy horticulturist bastard-child of Marie Curie and Timothy Leary. In all the books he found, no picture of Schultes showed him at anything other than the utterly concentrated pursuit of science and advancement of learning. It was difficult to find a photo of him with a smile on his face. He was never seen except in khaki work clothes and his jungle hat. It was hard to imagine him laughing, and if he did, Gerald knew it would be a doleful chuckle, acknowledging our failures, our frailties. Gerald saw that Schultes, like him, was a diarist and kept logs whose notations would become famous in their detailing of the exploits of a versatile intellect.

Gerald pored through pharmacopia and Amazon basin travel books. He learned the Latin names of the plants and reviewed the venation pattern of the dicotyledons. At the end of each evening Gerald closed his aching eyes, turned out the light and waited for rapture to roll his way, and it did, again and again, like a blessed mail delivery, a full envelope of enhanced reality. He found that if he fasted, something not specifically recommended but not prohibited in the protocol, the euphoria could be prolonged for most of the night. The jerkings of his legs calmed. His bed was dry. He felt different. He was reminded of a certain type of old guy who would wander into the office from time to time, *wanting* to buy insurance, always term-life. Margolese, who, for all his faults, could read people like brightly painted highway signs, told everyone in the office *not* to sell to these old men. He said these guys were *done* and that you could never indemnify against them because they had seen their futures, their ends. They were ghosts, Margolese would say. Gerald remembered that they had a certain dignity about them, a presence. They eyed Margolese as he patiently refused them their imminent payday, as though they were staring down the great white whale.

He imagined such a change in himself; he no longer looked like something found on a beach—pale and faintly organic, the scent of decay—but now appeared eminently at ease, and if the nurse taking his blood sample blew the vein, well, he would say, he had other veins. Desires dissipated in him, and any pangs of appetite that he harboured were relieved with each night of sleep. He smiled more. Jacqueline told him that he looked self-possessed, a compliment that he accepted with an equanimity that the self-possessed have in such abundance. He had to admit to himself that he had become faintly magnetic and was looked to when the group went out to restaurants or bars: Jacqueline habitually sat across from him, as she was this night, her leg occasionally brushing against his under the table. She blushed while her sister fended off Chuck's clumsy advances.

Ivan asked Gerald about insurance, that was his business, wasn't it? To which Gerald said he no longer had an opinion on its sale or purchase, but supposed it was necessary for some people. How did they feel about bio-pimping? Ivan continued, now animated; it was a word he had seen in the paper, describing what they did, becoming subjects for phase one studies. There was a pause before Gerald admitted that he had never heard the word. He considered in silence that he could not answer the question as the money now seemed so foreign, so beside the point, that it was like asking about the cash value of motherhood or the retail price of peace of mind.

Carolyn left after Chuck got up to use the washroom, whispering something to Jacqueline as she prepared her escape. Jacqueline stayed; would Gerald give her a lift? It wouldn't be a problem. It was not lost on Gerald that since he achieved this inner state of calm and abandonment of earthly desire, Jacqueline was attracted to him. But where this paradox would have tortured him before, it only amused him now. He was relaxed and happy as she held onto his arm and climbed the stairs to his place. He had promised her coffee. Gerald showed her the apartment, before slovenly and bare but now ascetically appealing, unadorned, minimalist, a place Schultes could have rested before he disappeared into the jungle.

They sat on the couch and drank coffee, listening to the city outside. They talked. Her parents were from Hong Kong, she said, Kowloon, precisely, and had decided to emigrate when their daughters were in high school, wishing the security of distance in the event that the Chinese considered the 1997 takeover as an opportunity for ideological re-education. She and her sister had stayed to continue at university when their parents chose to return after the takeover passed without more than fireworks and handshakes. She told Gerald that she was the younger sister by seven minutes, and while this didn't seem to be a big deal to most—a twin was a twin, after all —she explained that in her family birth order imposed a hierarchy more important than the mere fact that they were identical. There were no sons, she said, taking a sip from her coffee cup and pausing. Carolyn was number one. She didn't mind.

Gerald told her about himself, self-conscious for a moment, hoping she wouldn't ask where the dog was. He listened to himself and felt as though he were describing a third person, not a bad guy, middle child of a normal family that he didn't see much of now, for reasons he didn't really understand. He had a sister and a brother, both of whom were married and well on the way to what he supposed was considered happiness. His mother, he told Jacqueline, had always labeled him a happy baby, not a crier, not much of a bother at all. His father left the family when Gerald was a child and was remembered from a photograph that Gerald kept. The photo showed his father fishing, oblivious to his picture being taken, his facial features shadowed by the brim of a straw hat. That was all the emotion he could summon up about his father, he said, no ill will or desire for a reunion. Just a man in a hat.

He worried at first that by telling her such things he would be seen as overly nostalgic, which he felt he wasn't, but he had recently given his childhood much thought, and not about what went right or wrong, but what he imagined was the course of it. How odd it all seemed. How sweet. His mother had bags of photographs— from which pictures of his father had been quietly expurgated— that she would spill on the kitchen table and the family would rummage through: red-faced at the beach, Halloween, the kids arranged on the couch at home. Leafing through the pictures, his mother reminisced about her children: his brother Robert's athletic skill or his sister Margaret's intelligence. She always spoke fondly of Gerald's contentedness.

"Are you happy now?" Jacqueline asked.

"I think so," he said.

She kissed him and for the first time in his life he did not experience desire in its restrained increments but rather felt only the lightest touch of her lips on his, a moment of taste, the faintest edge of a tongue against his upper teeth.

They lay in bed throughout the night, both perfectly at ease in the understanding that Gerald's protocol forbade intercourse, and that the drop in the sperm count of the weekly semen analysis would draw suspicion. His thoughts drifted to what he had said earlier, speaking of his mother and imagining himself in his crib, smiling and playing with the corner of a blanket. He closed his eyes and felt bliss, not knowing if it was because of the medication or Jacqueline beside him. Shadows rose along the river he floated down: familiar people stood like trees along the banks, waving photos from their hands. A hat floated by. In the morning he awoke alone.

PHANTASTICA

The weeks that followed were the happiest of his life. Thoughts of annuities and term life policies evaporated as though Margolese had been a meteorological system stalled above him that only now had been replaced by fair weather. He saw the rest of his group often, as they waited for their various examinations at the Institute's test centre. One day near the end of the protocol's final week, after producing his sample in private and awaiting the phlebotomist for his second, he looked up from a new biography of Schultes and spotted Jacqueline reading in a recliner, recovering from a liver biopsy she had undergone that morning. He caught her attention and they looked at each other from across the room, sharing something unaffected by distance, unmediated by touch.

She shifted in her chair and he thought that she was going to get up, but she repositioned herself and kept reading. He settled into his plump leather chair, closed his eyes and thought of himself in Schultes' khakis, searching for a species of Mexican marigold, sniffing the unpolluted air of the new world. In his dream he floated down the wide and silent river with what he had collected, absorbing every magnificent shade and sound and letting this fecund, wonderfully rotting world diffuse through him. He achieved such a state of contentment, such marrow-saturating pleasure, that when it was finally shattered it was as though the water's surface had been rent by a predator's lunge.

The sound of a melee had erupted down the hall: a crash, voices raised, then a silence, followed by a more general cacophony. Someone yelled to call the police as he and Jacqueline came upon a crowd of people, a hydra of limbs pulling and twisting. Gerald caught a glimpse of the melton sleeve of a hockey jacket and then a mouth, contorted and rimmed with frothy spittle. He had seen a seizure once in the supermarket, witnessed the puckering of the woman's face, the scleral stare, then the grunt and convulsive fall—from which he had backed away in shock and shame, abandoning his cart right there as the woman writhed in the aisle. He could tell this was different when the bodies cleared and he saw Peterangelo, lucid and livid, restrained above Chuck's prostrate form.

Security guards materialized: two huge men in black who pretzelled Peterangelo into submission and hustled him away, frog-marching him to some exit or back room. Chuck staggered to his feet and immediately fell backward, arms splaying like the branches of a tree felled in the wind. Chuck was a face of blood; spatters from his mouth dappled his shirt and his eyes tried to maintain a focus, but failed and rolled back into the depths of his watery sockets. Somebody found a towel—towels were everywhere in the test centre—and pressed it against Chuck's face to sop the blood. Chuck regained his balance and sat up. Peterangelo had attacked him, he said to no one in particular, he had barged into the Test

Centre and wanted to see a supervisor and, finding no one, had confronted Chuck and accused him of being a mole. Then he clocked him.

"A mole?" Jacqueline said.

Chuck shrugged. His forehead wrinkled and he looked as though he would begin to cry at any moment. To everyone's relief he brought the towel to his eyes and lay back. A nurse arrived with a fresh towel and tended to him. There was half-hearted talk of calling an ambulance but after the supervisor arrived and assumed responsibility for Chuck's condition this was forgotten. Chuck would be attended to, it seemed.

That Friday, after their day was over at the Institute, Gerald and Jacqueline met Carolyn at the Spoon. Carolyn had first heard about the altercation between hypodermic punctures for some skin testing protocol she was freelancing. As the technologists distributed welts along her back, Carolyn listened to them marvel at how a lunatic as declared as Peterangelo could get back onto the property.

"I didn't think he was that crazy," Gerald said.

"Oh, you have a positive opinion of everybody," said Jacqueline, examining the margarita glass in her hands. "I don't think I can have this; I'm salt-restricted."

"Insane, apparently," Carolyn intoned as she carefully tried to position herself. "All the technologists at the Institute knew. The Security staff had been warned that he was volatile. They were waiting for him." She grimaced. "Did we have to get a booth?"

"He wasn't getting work," Jacqueline explained. "And we were all doing so well. It must have been difficult for him."

They talked about Peterangelo's attack. Gerald sensed relief at the table—Chuck had been his victim but it could have been any of them standing in the way of his train-wreck. They sat in silence considering that for a while, mentally running through transcripts of their conversations with Peterangelo, provocations building, slates being tallied in his diseased head.

Carolyn downed Jacqueline's abandoned margarita and they began to drink at a more committed pace. By the time Ivan joined them the alcohol had suffused their indifferent mood and they could not muster more than a few words among them.

"Hey," Ivan said to the nods of the others. He ordered a beer. "Rough day."

"You heard?" Jacqueline asked.

"That's what I've come to talk to you about," he said, lifting a briefcase onto the table and laying it flat. The spring-loaded latches popped open. To Gerald, who had not seen Ivan in the last week, there was something about the young man that made him seem older, more competent. Gerald thought that maybe he should buy a briefcase; he remembered seeing Schultes carrying one when he testified before the House Committee on Rubber and Guttapercha Production in the Amazon Basin.

"I didn't want it to end this way," Ivan said, shuffling papers and sounding very official, "but after speaking to our legal counsel…"

"Legal counsel? What's this 'our legal counsel'?" Carolyn asked.

"After what happened to Chuck—he fractured an orbital bone, you know—after what happened today at the Institute our legal counsel thought it best that the experiment end here and now."

There was an impressive, stupefied silence.

"It's our usual policy to disclose at the end of the study, of course. You'll still be fully compensated, by the way. The Institute feels very strongly about that."

" So Chuck wasn't a mole," Jacqueline said in such an innocent way that Ivan looked immediately wounded. She tipped back the last of her margarita.

"Uh, no, that was all Peterangelo's paranoia. No, no, Chuck's the real victim here. Peterangelo was rejected from the study. The Minnesota Multiphasic showed a spike in his skepticism indices that we only picked up on a secondary analysis, but it was enough to exclude him. Peterangelo got wind of the protocol, a former employee told him, he was upset of course, and I suppose he thought Chuck was the group invigilator and…"

"What was the study?" Gerald asked as though it mattered.

"Group dynamics protocol," Ivan said, straightening papers and passing the collated copies to the three of them. "We measure everything. The data we've amassed is really amazing, but we don't know how participation itself affects the subjects. A total wild card, an effect we try to control for but can't even define. This study was part of a meta-analysis. We need you to sign these release forms."

"And the medications?" Carolyn said.

"Inactive agents," Ivan said.

The release forms were as thick as the psychological profiles they had filled out weeks before, full of suffixes: -ee, -ant, -or. Gerald turned to the last page where his signature was needed. Carolyn and Jacqueline had already done the same. Once they'd signed, Ivan smiled and shut his briefcase.

"I'm sorry about this. I can see that you're disappointed and I understand," Ivan continued. "In the future we'll try to simplify these types of studies, but for now, well, we're still on the steep edge of the learning curve." He pulled the case off the table and paused for a moment in that way people do when they feel a vague aura of shame around them. He turned and walked out of the bar.

A silence settled as Ivan left. The waitress came over with Ivan's beer, and to see if they needed anything else. Carolyn waved her away.

"Who's going to pay for this?" the waitress said.

Carolyn opened her fist and a crumpled bill dropped to the table. The waitress placed the glasses, veined with dried beer foam and salty margarita residue, on the tray, and gave the table a hurried wipe with three successive circles of her cloth. They all leaned back, even Carolyn. It was time to go. Gerald said goodnight to Carolyn and Jacqueline in the parking lot and drove away, assuming that no one wanted the additional embarrassment of company.

Four tablets, biconvex, scored, light blue. Gerald wondered how much sugar there was in each one and how they must have laughed their asses off at the Institute when they fabricated their phony protocols. He didn't realize that he had reflexively taken one of the pills until it was in his gullet with a swallow of water from the tap. He put the rest into the sink and watched the water dissolve them. Outside the city hummed and in the distance lines of traffic snaked toward the midtown bridge. Gerald turned off the light and found comfort at the thought of Schultes' disappointments, which were not many, but were well known: the rubber plant cultivation failure, the government's indifference to his post-war work. If he had been diminished by these setbacks it had not been apparent. Gerald closed his eyes and thought of the rivers that Schultes had traveled. He thought that with each stroke of his paddle and every footfall in the jungle, Schultes would be a different man, someone closer to the man he would eventually become. As the river narrowed and the roof of vegetation thickened over Gerald, the sounds became louder, and he felt as if they were emanating from deep inside his chest. Further and further he sank, Schultes sitting behind him in the canoe, wearing his trademark hat and using his paddle as a rudder to guide them into the deepening darkness. Gerald felt the sediment weigh upon him, compressing his body into something elemental, tiny and purely insignificant, pushed by the flow of the river to where it would open on the light of a new world.

Lumière

or

*An Accounting of the Events of December 28th, 1895, at the
Grand Café, Boulevard des Capucines, Paris*

1

With André-Philippe still not yet arrived it was left to me to inform Gaston that it would not be a formal evening of dining for the private party, that Monsieur Saupin had not even planned for *entrées* to be served. Gaston, although the *sous*, has a temper worthy of a kitchen master; he cursed and flung a pot to the floor. (A true chef would never treat a pot in this manner, it would be an apostate act). He shouted in a most theatrical way that he was under the impression that this was still a restaurant with a duty to prepare food. "These people, these *exhibitionists*," he said, pronouncing his words with deliberation and tender hatred, as though overcooking an egg for an enemy, "do they not eat? Do they not *breathe*? They should be told to go to a burlesque house. For all I care, they can show their wares in the brothels." Gaston is, to be kind, a difficult man, but he plays an integral part in the operation of the kitchen and as the maître d'hôtel it is my duty to forge his personality with every other one in the kitchen to create a thing of beauty. Something of true, if only transient, beauty. Didier has acknowledged this talent of mine, hailing me as 'maestro' on several occasions when the elements of our little orchestra require a firmer-than-usual hand. On this occasion I nod solicitously at Gaston, and with a practiced look of shared concern on my face I back out through the kitchen doors.

53

2

Under the circumstances, Monsieur Saupin wishes to have the restaurant continue in as much of a habitual way as possible. It is the busiest time of the year and to close down even a part of the restaurant is madness, but Monsieur Saupin has been taken by the idea and cannot be moved. He told me that *le groupe Lumière* will be seated in a large room off the Grand Salon. This area is ideal for private parties as it can be cordoned off from other parts of the restaurant and it even has its own wrought-iron stairway, useful for those patrons who do not wish to make their attendance a matter of public note. The large room off the Grand Salon has also been chosen because its huge dormers are shuttered and it is here that the light can be most easily blocked. The need for discretion—the shuttered hall, the disclaiming of any collation, the possibility of boots clambering up back stairways—has aroused interest, and some concern, in all employed at Le Grand that the activities to occur here are, to say the least, potentially unsavoury. The staff are proud to attend to—indeed, to cultivate—the individual tastes of our patrons, and while we implicitly trust Monsieur Saupin not to bring the restaurant into disrepute, I had to admit to *le gérant* that they are upset that no meal will be served, as the evenings before *Jour de l'an* are amongst our busiest and the gratuities bestowed are very much in keeping with the generous spirit of the festive week. No one can imagine gratuities being dispensed in a darkened room, from patrons who have not been fed. Monsieur Saupin flushed when I raised this point during our review of the dinner menu for the other patrons. He took a moment to collect himself—during which I feared for my position, for it could be considered that I was overstepping the bounds of propriety—before saying that arrangements had been made and anyone serving this party would be more than adequately rewarded.

3

It is late morning before I can relax; my first rest since daybreak. The café is nearly empty save for the party at table 14 lingering over their long-emptied cups, given over to that feeling of having stayed in each other's company for too long yet not knowing quite how to disperse. The waiters glare professionally at them from a safe distance. I do not mind these stragglers though, nor do I mind the waiters' disdain for them, because it occurs to me that all of this seems perfectly logical for this time of the morning. Once I would have said that such a moment was supposed to appear this way, that it was *intended*, but Didier has convinced me that saying such things is old-fashioned. He has taken upon himself to educate me in the ways of the great philosophers, like our countryman Henri Bergson, a name I did not recognize two months ago but whose work Didier swears will change my life, despite my assertion that I need no such changes. Nonetheless, Didier has given me his copy of Bergson's work. I am flattered by his thinking that I have an appreciation for such things—my experience comes not from the lycée but from the daily placations of the hungriest of Parisian intellectual society—but Didier tells me that this work is being read by men like me, even carried about in the coat-pockets of stewards and clerks, read by fire and furnace light. Didier gets rather animated when he speaks like this and I try not to show embarrassment at being herded in with the mechanics and clerks. The book is interesting though, the parts of it I can make out, full of words like *tension* and *psychology* and German words that I refuse to even understand. So let me rephrase, *à la Bergson*, that this is not the way the café was intended to look at this moment, but rather, this is the way a café appears to me, at half-eleven, halfway between Christmas and the end of the year. Flakes of pastry. The smell of coffee. Almonds. The chill of winter held at bay. I breathe it in, all of it, a wide world of sensation. No intention, only sensation. I have a moment to exhale before Didier asks me about what he perceives as the unusual smell of *les moules* and whether or not I can locate an extra hundred chairs for *le groupe Lumière*.

4

André-Philippe arrives at two, having spent his morning at the markets. He has a list of deliveries, all of which will arrive before five when he will set to work. He is unhappy, but not in the sputtering, irascible way that Gaston is; rather, he is melancholic over the state of fish and fowl from which he has had to make selections. Our André-Philippe is a true artist, and on days when he has been asked to paint from a palate of greys, he suffers, and we share in it with him. His moods find their way into his food. The béchamel will have a lingering broadness tonight. The patrons suffer gloriously with him; his passion is accepted as a measure of his artistry, the kitchen his Gethsemane.

5

The Lumière party begins to arrive at two o'clock. They have an entourage the size of which I have only seen accompanying visiting dignitaries or our more beloved stage performers. For some reason the Lumière brothers refer to the young men in their group as 'engineers'. Four of these so-called engineers carry a large wooden crate with great care through the main hall and up to my station. Behind them another member of the group saunters in: a tall man with a metal bar hooked at the end like a shepherd's staff hanging from the crook of his arm. He sniffs at the surroundings as though he were a general surveying the dimensions of a battlefield. For a moment I cannot tell if he is with the other engineers and I prepare to ask if I can assist him, but at that moment he smiles and claps another of the engineers on the back. The metal staff is handed to another, perhaps a subordinate, and they proceed past me, following Didier to the large room off the Grand Salon. Their long coats are filthy, hemmed with the discolouration of sweat and oil, and seeing them enter rouses in me the urge to bar their entrance further, for what is the maître d'hôtel if not the protector, the benevolent despot of his realm? But then I remember the words of Monsieur Saupin, that there will be a rich reward for all of us, for the reputation of the café itself, once the evening is over. I must trust him.

The Lumière brothers leave after an hour. Their smiling faces tell me that they are satisfied with the preparations. They stand on the steps outside the café for several moments, as though studying the afternoon sky. It is the colour of flatware in a sink of water. It is a haze that promises snow.

6

The Lumière brothers return at half-six amid considerable excitement. Didier, who is from Lyon and who has relatives working in the Lumière factory there, whispers to me as Louis and Auguste pass us. Louis is the younger but the more formidable of the two. Didier tells me that he invented a photographic process while still in his teens that turned his parent's Lyon studio into a flourishing industrial concern. It is said that what the world knows of France is known through the plates of *les Frères Lumière*. Auguste limps somewhat, but still has a commanding presence in his own right.

7

As my attentions are fully focused on my duties elsewhere in the restaurant I am able to supervise the seating of patrons in the large room off the Grand Salon. It appears that there is a group loitering around the large entrance doorway and I at first assume that the doorway has not yet been opened. It is then, remembering the importance placed on this occasion by Monsieur Saupin, that I venture over to see if I can be of assistance. The door, however, has been opened and those at the entrance are there because the room is already fully occupied.

8

It is unnatural to see the room so dark, even on a late afternoon in winter. I cannot see how many have come to this gathering but assume there are a hundred souls in the room, which is as dark and cold as a cave. A light flickers on the far wall and for a moment

I assume that Didier or someone else has started a fire in the fireplace. It is not a fire.

9

It is as though a wave passes through us, as though we are standing on a pier and are swept away. I see the movement of heads, a set of hands flies up, people turn to run and in a moment I am outside the door, sprawling under patrons who exclaim to God that this cannot be happening. I lift myself to my feet and re-enter the room, pushing past onlookers, because I am the maître d'hôtel and until Monsieur Saupin arrives I am responsible for whatever is provoking this mayhem.

10

It is women. Spectral women. Forms that hover and move, stepping out of a door that opens. Yes, from that darkness these women emerge. Cheers erupt from the crowd and a man at the front of the room walks up to these moving women, placing his hand on the courtyard dust that they walk upon, as though wishing to touch them. *C'est fou*, he knows it as well as I do, but he cannot bring his hand down. He runs his hand over the courtyard floor and seems surprised to find a wall there. He pats the wall tenderly and then thumps it as if angered that it will not yield the touch of these simple women, angered that it is still just a wall. He turns to the crowd, stupefied. More cheers. Uproar. Then the light is on him and he is in covered in the courtyard dust, the hems of skirts brushing over his face, *his* face, which we can still plainly see. I can see him through the movement of these women and then I think that these are certainly ghosts and that I must avert my eyes to save my eternal soul, but I cannot look away.

11

Blackness. Silence for a moment and then tumult. Shouts for Louis and Auguste to explain themselves. The lamps are lighted. The relief of the gas flame and the familiar shadows it casts. The largest shadow cast is that of Louis who stands at the front, arms in the air to silence the uproar. For a moment I feel that all this is beyond my abilities to control. Where is Didier? I look for him as Louis clears his throat. I pray that he will clear the room. A broad smile crosses his face. *Mesdames et Messieurs! Encore, La Sortie des Usines Lumières!*

12
Hats are thrown into the air, their shadows like bats in momentary flight.

13
A large projected photograph, a grey square on the wall, in it another wall is seen, this with a set of doors. At the right edge of the picture there is the most miraculous thing, movement of leaves, waving so, so like a tree that I look for the continuation of its branches in the darkness that borders it, and when I cannot see it I feel a despair and exhilaration that I only remember from childhood.

14
The doors swing open to gasps and applause. From the darkness the women move again, turning to the right and left. One of the women looks at me and I turn my eyes to the ground, embarrassed to see a peasant woman dressed such as this, caught unawares.

15
I cannot stay. I glance around to see all in the room are held rapt. Didier has reappeared, beside me, tears on his cheeks. I cannot stay. I turn to him and he brushes them away. *I miss Lyon*, he says, not taking his eyes off the screen.

16
The sixth time it is as though we are listening to a familiar piece of music. The ghosts are no longer threatening but now enchant us.

We watch their graceful movements, uncommon for peasant women, and sigh as it ends.

17

The engineers work furiously on the machine, the *cinématographe*, as Louis Lumière calls it, trying to bring other images from it. There is silence as Lumière stands at the front of the hall, *Et maintenant, L'Arrivée d'un Train en Gare de la Ciotat!* I have no idea what he means.

18

I cannot breathe. The frantic movement of limbs obscures my view of the train that speeds towards us, hurtling through this wall to destroy the café and consume everyone inside. I am knocked off my feet but I see it, now from the side, as though we had been bodily thrown off the tracks. I can feel the steam, sense the impend-ing impact but nothing happens. The wall is black again and the train is gone, its burst of steam now a cloud somewhere else.

19

A comedy. A horse trotting. A world apart from anything we know. *There is a world where we thought there was nothing.* I want to say this to Didier but he is gone, pushing among the crowds thronging les Lumières, wishing to shake their hands, hoisting them high and carrying them on shoulders. "It is not real," a man behind me says out loud but to no one in particular, trying to convince himself of the proposition.

20

André-Philippe stands near the doorway, transfixed by the images that continue to fill up the far wall. To break the spell cast on me, I force myself to tell him that we must return to the dining room and kitchen. He looks at me vacantly, as though not knowing who I am.

21

The Grand Salon is full of people and kitchen staff straining to perceive the cause of this sensation. It is an effort to get through them but once I do I see the tables, abandoned food and glasses half-full, candles burning as though nothing had occurred. Aside from Gaston sitting at the back door smoking, the kitchen is empty, not a soul to witness pots still on the boil and the smell of meals imminently becoming cinders. It has been abandoned as though to an invading army.

22

Eventually the *cinématographe* is packed away and the Lumière brothers leave to a thunderous ovation. The diners return, stunned and perplexed, to their seats. They lift their utensils to address food that simply sits on the plate. A pall is cast. I can feel it as well. Even my clothes feel strange—ill-fitting, tight and loose at the same time—and while I am not in any way tired I am anxious to finish this evening's work. The kitchen is in disarray, Didier and André-Philippe are nowhere to be found. But Gaston remains steadfast in the kitchen, his contempt for the activities this evening well matched by his poor eyesight and so he has not been in the least tempted by the spectacle, not witnessed anything extraordinary tonight except his promotion amidst the mutiny of his confrères. He rages at the remaining kitchen staff who have drifted back to their stations, announcing to them through his hectoring the arrival of a new regime, a new age. Everything is different, even Gaston: he is now a happy man in this echoing kitchen. I check my watch. Monsieur Saupin will arrive soon. I don't know what to tell him.

Nightflight

Raymond knew something was wrong when the taxi driver asked him if they were getting close. He had been roused from a light, semi-drunken stupor to hear the words trailing off and he paused to think for a moment, as though some sober authority inside him was verifying what the driver had said.

Raymond tried to speak but started coughing instead and needed to sit forward. "The Bellcroft. I said the Bellcroft Inn." He looked out the side window into the rippling darkness of Vermont countryside.

"I told you I didn't know where it was," the driver replied, his eyes meeting Raymond's for an instant in the rear-view mirror. His head jerked nervously, as though he were trying to make his point face-to-face with Raymond.

"You took me as a fare," Raymond said, sitting up on the edge of the seat and trying to peer through the darkness. It made him feel ridiculous. "How long have we been driving?"

"About forty-five minutes. You were going to tell me when we got close."

"Oh, Christ. Stop the car."

The driver's head toggled in position as though he had heard the command but the car continued at an unchanged rate down the road. Raymond's anger and confusion gave way to fear. The command to stop was as harsh a denunciation as a taxi driver could ever hear and now the man's twitches seemed not pitiable but ominous. Raymond couldn't even remember seeing an illuminated sign on the car's roof, he had just got into the next car in line once the reception was over. In the back seat, an expanse of vinyl as wide as a park bench made him feel small and easily ignored, and he was not particularly relieved to finally hear the indicator's tocking as the muted green light pulsed in the darkness of the dashboard. No one was on the roads at this time of night, he thought, and the act of signaling had an odd deliberateness to it, something pathologically calm, and it froze him. He began to panic profusely, imagining a frenzied chase through the whiteness of the headlights followed by this lunatic, feeling the underbrush tear him as his lifeless body was dumped into a ditch. Vermont could be deadly.

"Stop the car," he said again, calmly, as though talking someone back from a ledge.

The driver pulled the car off to the side of the road. He sat motionless with both hands on the wheel, the correct ten and two positioning. Raymond cleared his throat, unsure what came next now that the vehicle had stopped and the threat of volatility seemed passed, or at least less imminent. The indicator counted a heartbeat half of his own. The driver put his head to the wheel and for a moment more Raymond thought about his options, of just opening the door and leaving, of becoming that type of person who simply leaves cabs. There were, however, subsidiary issues: night-time navigation in rural Vermont, hindered by an extra vodka-rocks and complete spatial disorientation, the embarrassment of the thought of death by exposure, the hundred graceless exits of an autumn night in the back-country. The door remained unopened however, as Raymond found himself leaning forward to touch the driver's shoulder. The man was weeping.

"Look, it's no big deal, we'll come to a crossroads and then we'll have our bearings. Besides, I think the Bellcroft is on the road to Hyde Park." The man was unconsoled.

"It's not that."

Well then, Raymond thought, taken aback at the curtness of the driver's correction, what the hell is it? Is this therapy, then?

Some sort of work-release program for aspiring taxi drivers?

"Look, bud..."

"Allen."

"Allen. Get to your dispatcher and just ask him for directions." The years of living on the Upper East side—and the inherent, constant exposure to taxi-driver personality disorder—was paying off for Raymond, easing him into survivalist mode like it was a default setting.

"I don't have a radio. This is a private car. I just do this part-time." He pinched his nose with a tissue that he peeled off a larger wad. He honked and wiped.

"Do you know the area?" Raymond asked.

"No. I'm from Rutland."

Raymond sank back into the seat. He was exhausted. His muscles ached mysteriously, as though effort had been extracted without his consent. The night had not gone well; Lorraine had left for their bed and breakfast hours ago. God only knew if *she* got home. And the celebration of his parents' anniversary, with the ostentatious expanse of the tent and the jazz band, only worsened his mood. He felt alone at the party, and once Lorraine left he found himself looking at his parents as they sat at the head table until they seemed to him like imposters, wearing familiar masks, incorporating mannerisms flawlessly, but somehow not his mother or father. After his parents moved to Vermont and restored their Federalist cottage, they seemed to change, appropriating lives from architecture magazines and home gardening shows, seamlessly indoctrinating themselves into a genteel cult life of fresh air and artificially distressed chairs. His father took to wearing plaid shirts and stopped registering, or at least expressing, contempt for those around him. His mother seemed happier too, developing an almost Buddhist calm as she considered every angle of their tiny new box house, a fraction of the size of the one they vacated in Westchester. They were happy now, after years of recriminations and a trial separation when Raymond was a sophomore at Cornell. They stayed together, and it seemed as though the years of difficulties and conflicts had polished them into, if not identical, then complimentary, placid partners. And yet their newfound happiness seemed so false that Raymond had difficulty visiting them, which was just as well as the restored house could barely contain the happy couple and led them to concoct the idea of the tent for their thirty-fifth anniversary celebration. He hated tents: the probationary atmosphere, the marquee tawdriness, and tonight he chafed at the canvas swaddling him like a shroud. The gaiety was oppressive, with relatives wagging flutes of Veuve-Cliquot and talking of summer places with restricted access. The tent had been full of family: cousins, aunts and uncles, all variations on a genetic theme. He could detect among many in the crowd the common features of eyes a touch too close and the prognathic Irvine profile, among the other traits of overdrinking and morbid self-reflection. He was only too happy to have his older sister Didi give the toast; by that time Lorraine was long gone and he had committed himself to a more advanced regimen of vodka tasting. His frequent trips to the bar, along with the night air, imparted a roguish vigour on him. Didi told him he was stinking and asked him where the hell Lorraine was. Maybe his legs hurt from all that walking to the bar. He remembered the relief at seeing some unfamiliar faces and smiled at some of the young women gathered at tables near the periphery of the tent. Outside one of the portable toilets he sidestepped his cousin Michael, who had been busy all evening announcing the windfall he made investing in a technology company whose product or function no one, including the investor himself, seemed able to explain. Back inside, the band had started another set. People danced through the amber light of the tent.

"I've been to Rutland." Raymond said to Allen, almost reflexively.

"Oh yeah? You ski?"

"No. It was on business."

On a clear October afternoon, the landing gear of a small plane had clipped the very tops of a cedar grove that lined the Rutland

Municipal airport. The pilot brought it in too low, that much could be surmised from the height of the clipped trees and where the plane eventually hit. It was one of Raymond's first assignments and because of this he was given the grunt-work assignment of doing the measurements. He stood out in the rain, tape measure in his hand, and put the distance at three hundred and forty-six feet five inches. The pilot—Caucasian male, thirty-five, good health, toxic screen negative—had less than fifty hours of solo experience. The conditions that saw the single-engine plane try to recover before ceding into a bank, then a roll, and then into the ground, were ideal. As far as Raymond could recollect they signed out the case as pilot error.

"Who do you work for?" Allen asked, gaining composure.

"National Transportation Safety Board."

"Is that Civil Service?"

"Yeah. I suppose."

The admission made Raymond uneasy. People still had certain preconceptions about civil service jobs. When he was more specific and told people he was a crash investigator, they would simply nod, thinking that he was the man they saw on the news, holding up the battered flight and voice-data recorder for the television cameras, that all that was necessary in an investigation was to open the black boxes and listen to the final minutes of something gone terribly wrong. He usually didn't take the time to explain that he was a small craft specialist, and that the light planes flying into the smaller airports had no black boxes or tower surveillance so that any crash was essentially an examination of evidence at the crash scene. He and his team, two other investigators and technical backup at the NTSB regional laboratories, would be dispatched to the site where they would collect information about the weather conditions surrounding the crash and the pilot variables. Next, they would examine the plane, essentially performing an autopsy on the craft, removing the gauges and display lights and dissecting the mechanics.

At one time he had been determined to become an aviator. When he first started flying lessons he thought about the different careers and found the solitary life of a bush pilot the most appealing to him. He pictured himself night-flying float planes through the wilderness of northern Quebec, with the glow of the avionics equipment and hum of the engines as his companion. He read St. Exupéry and studied the maps that showed the early mail delivery routes that stretched from Paris to Dakar and then across the ocean to Patagonia. Even phonetically, 'aviator' had something that 'pilot' lacked. You could pilot a shopping cart around the aisles of a supermarket. A dinghy could be piloted.

Things were different now, though, and by the time he had his pilot's license, the only jobs left to consider were in the shadowy corporate world of the small air carriers. Since deregulation in the early eighties, small transport companies had multiplied and made obsolete the single plane operations so that Raymond's dream disappeared as suddenly as St. Exupéry over the Mediterranean. He had no interest in hauling for the smaller carriers who he could see were cutting costs to preserve a margin, because he knew what the cost would come to. The move to the NTSB was natural once the planes began to disassemble in midair for lack of anyone paid to see to their maintenance. The work fascinated him in a way that made it seem almost perverse to sift through failure to find a cause for something that every pilot feared, something quite possibly beyond their control. There were other satisfactions—more than would be expected from simply closing the book on an accident, or drawing attention to insufficient industry standards—and it was something that his parents or Lorraine or Didi could never fully appreciate. He had difficulty explaining to people how the job changed him, how it allowed him to see that every disaster had a starting point and a trajectory, that there was a series of events that led to a moment of irreversibility and complete failure. A rivet loosened, a flange flapped, and a complex machine began to unzip itself, by degrees becoming what it was, assuming its native state and a condition of lower energy, returning to the ground.

The engine idled and Allen appeared to be searching for something. He was a big man, judging from the size of his shoulders and his posture in the driver's seat. Raymond patted his jacket, thinking that he had his cell phone in a pocket but nothing was there.

"Where do you think we are?" Raymond asked.

"No idea."

"Should we just keep going? We might find a phone booth."

"Yeah, yeah," Allen said, turning off the indicator and putting the car into gear.

The road passed under them like the back of a great animal, writhing in and out of the headlights. The stars were visible from the passenger window and Raymond thought he recognized a constellation as he glimpsed collections of stars through the tops of the trees. He hoped that Lorraine was safe and felt uneasy about letting her go back to the B & B earlier that evening. She had been tired after the trip up from New York and after the dinner, when the conversation between their table-mates faltered, she yawned. Raymond happened to be watching her at this moment and the sight of his wife yawning terrified him. After she took her hand away from covering her mouth, he noticed how the lower lids of her eyes glistened with the tears welled there. He could not tell her but he felt an inexplicable fear, not a sense of foreboding but something deeper and less random. He felt it was a moment that he could see her, a moment of clarity, and in this moment she seemed completely inured of him. She smiled and told him that she was going to take the car back to the bed and breakfast and he, alarmed by the casual gesture with which she declared boredom with her life, could not tell her that he needed her to remain there.

He hoped he would feel better once she was gone but his discomfort only worsened, the vodka having the opposite effect and heightening his senses. The tent crackled with sound: words he could not make out, voices billowing into white noise. He closed his eyes but saw his wife with her hand to her mouth.

"You okay now Allen?"

"Sure. Yeah. Hey look, I'm sorry about everything."

Now hitting a long stretch of straight road, Allen turned around. His eyes were red-rimmed and the lower lids puffy; to Raymond they looked like auxiliary mouths, little ones, each holding a great gumball of an eye. Raymond shrugged and then lifted his chin to indicate that he would appreciate Allen's full attention being focused on the asphalt ahead of them.

"Why are you so upset?" Raymond asked.

Allen looked at him through the rear-view mirror. "It's nothing."

"I'm sorry. That was a personal question."

Lorraine often chastised his tendency to ask questions of complete strangers, which he took as a compliment. Once, after attending the funeral for his wife's aunt, Raymond left the crowd milling around the doors of the memorial chapel and wandered off to find two men digging a grave. He stopped and asked them how long it took to dig a grave properly and if they really had to go six feet down. At first the two men thought he was a wise-ass or someone from a government agency, but they soon realized that he was genuinely interested. One of them, a huge black man with a right eye made milky by a cataract and who introduced himself as Clyde, told Raymond there were strict rules about depth, state regulations; and that while the job was generally enjoyable, it was more difficult in the winter when the earth cooled and became rock-hard. The other man, who did not bother telling Raymond his name, bragged that he had just helped exhume a body for the coroner's department.

"It's funny though," Allen said, as though he wanted to continue talking.

"What?"

"When I said. "It's nothing', it's sort of true," Allen said, now staring ahead as they passed a sign directing them to North Hyde

Park. "I got a depression. The doctor says it's due to nothing in particular. He said that depression is different now and it doesn't have to be because of something anymore."

"Oh yeah, like brain chemicals and stuff."

"Exactly. Hey, you depressed too?"

"No," Raymond replied.

"I was waking up at four in the morning and I wasn't eating and I was anxious all the time," Allen said, and Raymond wondered what sort of low-balling HMO he had if he was forced to continue driving private cars around and weeping at the wheel. "It still gets to me, now and then. Less since I've been on antidepressants."

"Yeah, you better now?"

"I think so. It's slow, though. I thought something would be at the bottom of it, but there wasn't anything there."

But Allen was right, he thought, it *was* odd, and frightening in a way, that something as black and enveloping as depression could just descend without a cause. He looked at Allen's head. Somewhere in Allen's brain something had happened: a memory, a chemical, a sadness blossomed. It would push him to wake up early or stop talking or step off a bridge. It happens. Raymond had, at one time or another, considered his mother to be depressed; she was a woman given to periodic and lengthy turns in bed followed by over-enthusiastic appearances at charity functions, forever with a glass in her hand. His father, if he was depressed, sought solace in the therapeutic effects of battering his family with the volume of his voice, and serial infidelity. Now they lived in Vermont and were happy. He could not dispute it nor for a moment comprehend it.

Parts of the road now seemed familiar, a ridiculous notion to Raymond as the darkness and the speed of the car made everything fade and shift and nothing could be recognized. He longed to be in a strange bed with his wife, with someone who inexplicably loved him and whom he loved, someone who slept, waiting for him. For a moment he felt as though he were above the trees and the rural roads and in the air again, quiet under the stars, engines shut off and simply drifting. He thought of Lorraine lying in bed, of the body that shared space with his, and he yawned. The road was familiar, he knew they were close. His eyes followed the thickets along the side of the road—dark and undulating, without break or variation—until suddenly, two stunning green points of light appeared in the underbrush and then a flash of white rose up and out of the darkness to take the form of an animal rushing over the car and past his head. He looked back but saw nothing.

The Gap

The real problem is that no one knows how to operate a water-cannon anymore.

It's not even a month after I'm promoted to a posting in fraud that I get the middle-of-the-night call to be part of a supplementary squad involving every division in the department: vice, corporate crime, homicide, the works. We have to back up the crew at the barricades. It doesn't bug me to go back to the street, but the others, veterans who haven't been out from behind a desk in years, are all sweating over their Academy manuals, reviewing cordoning procedures and street control, proper use of baton and spray. This isn't to say that we're intimidated, but we know that if they need us, the situation is already desperate. The next call goes to the army reserves and who makes that call to the Governor, God only knows. For weeks we'd heard the rumblings that there could be another Seattle, but none of us believed it. Now we get out of the truck—and you can feel the size of the crowd. Movement. Currents in an ocean. And in all that I can't make out a single face. All I know is that they've got gas masks and procured their fair share of billiard balls. The balls make that clacking noise as they hit the cement, which is sort of soothing in a way. When one hits your shield it sounds like a car accident.

Move up, the commander screams at me, seeing blood now that he's had a couple of men go to hospital from what was supposed to be a routine crowd-control detail. A few scalp wounds—they bleed like stink—a broken arm, someone with chest pain: all so that fucking college kids can have their fun and dress in masks and Palestinian scarves, so that we can have a trade deal that gets us fifty different types of something we don't need and can't afford. *Move up and seal off the fence,* he shouts into a megaphone, the last word punctured by a clanging feedback squeal as a rock or something hits the rim of the megaphone. *Move up,* he roars, nothing now to power the voice except rage. There is a hockey puck at my feet. They're throwing hockey pucks.

It's not like we're on television either, we *are* television, becoming the images that we've already seen. We saw the crews from all over the world arrive, satellite dishes gaping skyward, cameras primed, waiting for the first fractures. They have it covered from every angle, the cable news outlet helicopters fighting for space with the city's tactical chopper above the main square. From that height they can see the usual fare of smashed windows and cars, all of it played out in my city, hosting the world to a festival of overturned objects, a city that wasn't consulted and doesn't want any part of it, not the shadowy honchos in the limousines or the nose-pierced wingnuts that scream at them. Our guys are shown arranged behind the fences, dressed in black riot gear, visored and anonymous, interchangeable and lined-up in a phalanx. They all use that word 'phalanx', most of them drawl it out, Boss Hog style. *Fay*-lanks. It's the only time they use it. On the other side of the fence they dance and wave their flags, wrap their faces in bandanas and bullshit each other that they're tight with Subcomandante Marcos as they pay for their hotel rooms with daddy's gold card. They strut, college kids. They preen, talking about justice, concepts of justice, as they loft cinderblock pieces at my paycheck-to-paycheck ass. I got a kid. I got a very clear conscience.

They told us we were needed for crowd management. 'Management' is history once the tear gas drops and water cannons have been powered-up. It's a choke-hold and you can't let go. Everything is hazy with the gas and fifty-yard stares. But I will not be moved because I live here; unlike most of them on the other side, this is where I will be when the smoke clears. The only thing this gathering brings my city is ten minutes on the news and a month of broken glass. With so much gas in the air, they had to turn off the air-conditioning at the conference centre, delay the start of the whole damn thing because they need their air conditioning.

The order is given again. I don't want to go to seal off the gap in the fence. It's an idiotic order, even I can see that; they're aiming the water cannon into the stupid frozen grin of the chain-link hole, the very place they are telling us to go. I try to turn back but the guys behind me, the *phalanx,* are moving toward the opening. I dig in my heels—I don't care who knows how I feel—I'm determined not to go into that clothes-washer of a situation but I am inched closer. A torrent of water and swinging limbs. Theirs, ours. Sometimes hard to tell which.

I can see the cut edges of the fence, lips peeled back and puckering, the whole length rippling like a sail, unseaming itself. The spray hits my visor and I have a hundred sparkling hells to deal with, a fly's death. I jerk back when, out of the froth, my partner gets grabbed by this arm, maniacal, sinews and veins like rivers of rage until I get my nightstick and smash the arm for it's owner. The fingers extend, just like they're supposed to do, letting go of my partner's vest. Show *that* in anthropology class, fuckko. A guy could get seriously laid with a hero's story and a cast like he's going to have.

A blast from the water cannon sucker-punches me, a horse-kick in the ribs. I'm in the wrong position, feet wedged under the edge of the concrete retaining wall, so that the stream bends me over, pushing me into the opening of the fence. My riot shield is caught by the blast and it wrenches my arm away from its socket. It's worse once I catch the full force. The stream is metallic and cold and has the air sucked out of it. Deep space. The water rips my helmet off, the chin-strap tears giving up another taste, metallic again, in my mouth. It is a roar, unremitting, tearing jacket and vest from my back, peeling layers from me as I gasp and shake in an effort to release my pinned legs from behind the thigh-high retaining wall. It batters me, an angry water-god taking me for a wheelbarrow race. Something more than water is on me now, pounding down; feet or arms, maybe the limb I've given an extra bend to, flapping its bad karma back at me.

The breath is squeezed out of me, leaving me panicked, taking those hiccupping gasps and I think about dying, cameras on me. Flailing now, clinging, refusing to be flushed, whipped around the bowl until my feet are freed and I am airborne, a salmon expecting the next bite will be the bear's, a burst of pain to my groin (am I pinwheeling? Do they have this on tape?) and then the asphalt gets a taste of me. A shoulder on fire, not-at-all dulled by the ice-water. Blue lights and the sudden burst of a pain that has no similarity to anything in this world.

Frothy meridians divvy up the sky. Mine. Not mine. Billows as the gas comes down, then a mist. Someone stands over me, drops me a rag and the soaked-in vinegar helps for a moment. Fog rolls in. Breathe. There is a mist on my face, cool and seeping through the rag and not at all the corrosive taste of tear gas or pepper spray. It's water. I don't feel any water on my chest though and I panic for a moment that my back has been broken. But I can feel my feet, I can move them, and then I realize what's going on: a cop's riot shield lies over my trunk, upside down and catching water droplets like a half-pipe. I don't remember how it got there or from where it came from.

A voice behind me shouts out that they are using rubber bullets. I've seen the marks these leave, the shades of plum and the livid welts. The devil's hickey. Saw a girl from Buffalo gasp for air after one caught her in the throat and her larynx closed in, saw the cops stand back and watch as the ambulance came, batons and shields at their sides, dumb pack mule stares, as though she was having an allergic reaction. Just a job, they say.

A guy who introduces himself as Gunter helps me to my feet and the undulating world takes another deep breath in. The skies darken and my head almost bursts with pain. I run my hand through my hair and am surprised to find my fingers return unbloodied. Gunter looks at the shield that I now hold, knows exactly to whom it belongs, and flashes a victory grin. *Polizei*, he says. A canister of tear gas hits the ground twenty feet away, making that sound at impact like a full tin of soup. It scrolls towards us. Gunter bends down and grabs the smoldering pot with his rag-covered hand. A choking cloudburst and another arc. More soup sounds, distant.

At the beginning of the day I could actually tell who was with what group, saw that it was a real gathering of the clans. The trade-unionists bussed in on the AFL-CIO dime hung out at the back, wary of it all but unable to hide their pleasure at being seen and heard somewhere other than a lost-cause lock-out. Beside them were the hard-liners, earnest and twitchy, straight from their mini-boot camps where they were taught theories of chain-link, the vinegar trick and how to present your hands so as to make restraint most difficult. Everywhere banners flapped: eco-protesters shouting about genetically modified food, women's rights coalitions, student groups, third-world debt forgiveness alliances, brick throwers, punks, onlookers. Once the shots were fired I ran like everybody else. Where the hell is Gunter from? People are everywhere, running into each other, but all scrambling, as if there is a place to go to.

Gunter emerges from the mist, supported by a small-framed woman who sports the arachnid stare of an authentic gas mask. I can't be sure of the direction but I assume they're coming from the fence, taken one of the punishments meted out at the chain-link. Every fifteen minutes I ask myself why I'm here, missing midterms, crawling around with the insect woman and Gunter, why I'm not listening and nodding to labour-leader speeches less than a mile away at the tent city but instead have gravitated to the point of conflict, soaked and staggering, listening to my brain hum in pain.

Any means possible—heard last night at dinner from a guy

who went on to say he intended to get a blow-job from a female representing every G-7 country here this weekend. Fight the power man. Stay away from the insect woman. Any means possible. I can't blame him or pretend I didn't think about it myself, trying to close my eyes in the tent city vibrating with that fantastic energy, that desire, sublimating urges into overly-roused choruses of Woody Guthrie songs and thinking all the time that this was where legitimacy was. Here. Under the stars. For the first time I was in love with my life.

I was told by a guy who had some training that the way to take down chain-link is to shake it down. *Push and pull.* Don't let go, because if the water hits you, the fence is all you have. But why would we want to hold onto something we were trying to shake down? I said, and he looked at me as if I were stupid or worse, some sort of wise-ass. Che-fucking-Guevera, shouting instructions to people, eyes out for television crews.

After coming to I felt like I was underwater, every sound a pressure wave, every movement a current that ran against my aching head. Now I'm standing in the riot, a lost man, but it comes back to me now, the feel of the fence, the adrenaline and the wild hydra-kick of bodies. A brick heavy in my hand. People rush by me now, rag-tag howling anarchists, waving their arms in the residue of the tear gas clouds. Eddy currents. Fun, fun, fun. The camera loves them and whatever legitimacy they bring. I follow, the first steps since Gunter pulled me to my feet, an omnivorous pain throughout my body, echoing with each heel-strike.

Some things are certain, even in a riot. We will lose today. Criminal records will be tagged to us. Parents will be called from jail cells and a silence will punctuate every word. We will lose but we will choose our loss, turn our Guernica into a Stalingrad, and we will bring this choice into every home before the sports and after the weather. Don't watch me, just watch. I'm ready.

The water-spray hits me and so I raise the shield, crouch under it. People scream, choking with the gas and the water-blast. An errant shot from the water-cannon careens off the shield and almost knocks me back to the pavement, but I advance. One of the anarchist kids staggers by, a mouth of blood leading him away from his fun. We are legitimate. I'm at the fence, facing nothing but the anti-climax of unmanned, oscillating chain-link. I consider climbing but would have to abandon my shield and would likely be shaken off to a second concussion, which I have resolved to avoid.

I follow voices to the action clotted at the wound of the fence. I expected good versus bad, lines drawn and positions clear but it's a gang fight and nothing more. The dialectics of the bench-clearing brawl. Someone takes a swing at me, not a riot-cop but someone in a security uniform—whoever, he is pumped-up, likely a body-guard for some generalissimo whose pants our bankers want to get into; but I brandish my shield like a gladiator, repelling the palooka, who is then knocked over by a horse brought into the fray to restore order. Note to civil authorities: horses do not necessarily restore order. The beast, eyes streaming and wild with the noise and madness, rears and takes off, rider in tow. Cheers. Toward the fence now, because this is where legitimacy lies, this intersection of time and place and circumstance. Just watch. I push the shield against a couple of riot cops, a tender, taunting gesture, hoping they see that it is one of their shields, and they show me they do recognize it by starting to swing their batons wildly, a frenzied wind-milling, as though I have presented them with the severed head of their leader. Seismic shocks now, someone thrown against me until I can feel the ligaments in my knees shriek, and then the water. For all their faults, these fucks sure know how to handle a water-cannon.

Cambodian Rock Song No. 4

I asked where the cows were and everybody looked at me as though I were crazy. Delvecchio the foreman pointed over to the vats. There was meat in them, liquefied and waiting to be shot into moulds of pimento loaf or more imaginative casings. It was my job, my new job, to circulate through the plant, scoop up the liquid meat in little baggies, and perform a fat-content analysis on each sample.

It was not a happy time to be working at the plant. There was no livestock at the packing-house because the operation was in the process of being gradually shut down. With the killing floor idled, they now only processed and packaged meats shipped in from other plants. Layoffs had gutted two full shifts and those still employed had a resigned look, that gaunt end-of-the-siege stare. When I showed up for my government-subsidized summer job fresh from university finals I was met with a seething contempt, immediate and communal.

I was made part of the Quality Assurance team, three guys—Ed and Steve and Gordie—who patrolled the plant measuring effluent *e. coli* and mouse droppings in parts-per-million. These three reveled in the fact that they chose to include me in their group despite the fact that I was hated, even by them. The Q.A. crew set themselves apart, commandeering a separate table in the cafeteria where I was given a chair and dealt a hand in some inane lunch-hour card game that I played with a disinterest that further estranged me from my tablemates. Conversation among us was spare. Topics were rationed as tightly as syllables and the world was dissembled daily in a ritualized loop of table-talk. There were arguments about sports and electronics equipment, periodic updates on mutual acquaintances from high school usually along a theme of mundane catastrophe: divorce, jail time, insurmountable credit card debt and whether or not some band or other had sold-out artistically. None of them ever talked about having any other job before the plant. It was easy to imagine them shedding their graduation gowns for packing house jump-suits, their lives continuing at the plant as though the job had been just another, prolonged intramural event.

On my second day, Ed asked me what I was studying and I told him about an introductory physics course I took, about how it was centripetal and not centrifugal force. I explained entropy to his blank, then smirking, face. The others seemed to find the laws of thermodynamics hilarious as well. By day three I was already calculating minutes: end of the shift, end of the week, end of the job. After a day of collecting liquid meat in doggie bags and inhaling atomized animals, I made the journey between the rows of margarine rendering tanks to my laboratory, slouching to duck the oily mist that hung in the air and shrouded the huge metal columns. I hated my job and my co-workers, and it was made clear to me that it was mutual. When I came out one afternoon to find the driver's side window of my old Toyota shattered and the stereo stolen, I looked around the parking lot expecting to find satisfied faces, almost needing to feel their glee at the sight of my misfortune. But I was alone.

I took to shouting fantastic obscenities made inaudible by the machine-roar. I cursed my more well-off friends who spent their summers travelling in Europe and was prone to dark, elaborate thoughts concerning their journeys: malaria was contracted, cathedrals collapsed, planes disappeared from radar screens. My wrath was limitless, my relief fleeting.

It was in my windowless laboratory—a cinderblock cell where I daily practiced the art of adding sulphuric acid to the meat slurry in order to accurately measure fat content—that I first heard "Cambodian Rock Song No.4." You have to hear this, a friend said, handing over a worn cassette as we drank beer in his basement the night before. He had just returned from Asia and had about him an easy glow of road wisdom and sexual satiety, that well-recognized traveller's patina that I wanted to take a blow-torch to, but instead had to satisfy myself by accepting his tape. If nothing else, his kind gift (which I had already calculated how far I could throw) would be a diversion, and I needed diversion.

I listened. I was hooked. The Cambodian Rock Songs were anonymously performed and untitled except for their numbers— 1 through 14—which made them seem even more exotic, like new elements, glowing and dense, added to the end of the periodic table. The master tapes had allegedly banged around southeast Asia, surviving napalm and Pol Pot, before dropping into hands of my travelling friend.

I listened to it at work on my Walkman, especially "Cambodian Rock Song No. 4". It was my solace. At first I thought it may have been more the noise than music, the relief of soft sponge headphones against my ears blocking out the humming of the plant. But I was wrong: it was something about the song. It opened with jangly, almost inadvertent guitar chords followed by a Hammond B3 wheezing in accompaniment. Then came the voices, heard in the background, not singing but talking in barely audible, conspiratorial Cambodian chitchat, as though fretting whether the Khmer Rouge was going to break down the door for some fresh skulls. I concentrated on the silences, certain I could detect other voices whispering in the background. Perhaps because of that straining to pick up the echoes of voices that may not have been there, the Cambodian rock songs seemed different with each play. More mysterious and frightening. More exhilarating. I wasn't as angry after that. I don't know why. I hated to think that I was so completely pacified with a little gift from my travelling friend. Whatever the reason, everything became easier for me afterwards. I went to work every day in that huge empty shell of a packing-house, listened to music, measured the fat and learned to play poker. Passing through each department as I collected my samples, I would stop and watch the activities around me, able to go unnoticed because my travels were part of a larger routine. I saw how the ladies in deli meat packaging shook the tingles out of their cold hands every minute or so, as though they were flicking away their minor discomforts. I witnessed all the intimacies of a work place, how people didn't so much get consumed by a routine as they sought comfort within it, dipping into their rituals like a warm bath. With time, I came to be able to read grimaces, to appreciate the signs of someone working through the pain of aching joints just as I could recognize the furtive, twitchy routine of the slacker or the signs of contempt of a short-timer like myself. I became like a voice in the Cambodian rock songs, murmuring away, a ghost realizing he has become a ghost.

The plant itself still frightened me, but it had become beautiful too. It was an awesome place in the evening, emptied like a carcass, a huge thorax ribbed by ventilation shafts and conduits. In its echoing main hall, I would look around and could only think of the second law of thermodynamics, the movement of energy; that everything was breaking down and emptying out, and that we could only temporarily forestall it, reassembling ourselves until we began to fall apart again.

By August they had announced more firings at the plant. People no longer played cards at lunch but sat in silence, chewing and mentally dividing their severance pay by their monthly expenditures. Ed, who everyone knew drank too much, showed up at work with plum-coloured bruises under each eye. There was talk of a two-six, a car, and a tree. Now he took the bus to work. Steve said nothing but Gordie laughed and told him he looked like a raccoon. Ed reached across the table and soon the two were on the floor, sprawling among upturned chairs and shocked, expectant onlookers.

Driving home that day, I saw Ed at the bus stop. He tried for a moment not to make eye contact, but I was intent on giving him a ride and he finally accepted. He told me where he lived and when I said I knew the neighbourhood, he seemed surprised.

I wanted to play the tape for Ed, to have "Cambodian Rock Song No. 4" kick in like an auditory ipecac, slapping him on the back like it did for me. I wanted it to wake him up, to let him know that somewhere, somebody had been disobeying the second law, creating something from nothing, telling the powers that be that they would have to wait to polish his skull. There was still music left to make. I actually rummaged around the scattering of cassettes on the little shelf under the dashboard before remembering the jagged wound on the dash where the radio and tape player used to be. Wires splayed out from the hole; an argument cut short.

"Heh, heh. Upgrading the sound system are ya,' professor?"

"Yeah," I mumbled, being caught too off-guard to tell him to shut his mouth. Ed produced a smile from under his mask of twin shiners and continued to snicker, savouring his joke like a mouthful of that night's first beer. The chance to tell him to shut up came and passed me by again. Instead, I drove Ed home in silence. The plastic that covered the broken window began to ripple in the wind, making a high-pitched whistling noise that continued until I came to a stop at the next intersection and tore the cover off.

dollyclocks

From the atrium's balcony, Phillip looks down at Kenny wandering through the sculpture garden and asks himself what the title of *this* work would be, if he were allowed or so inclined to name the small boy.

Kenny reaches up with his right hand to touch the pieces of art that appeal to him: the corrugated floating pieces of a mobile or anything brightly coloured. It is a busy hand, one that has already been thrust indiscriminately and against Phillip's repeated warnings through the opened window of an uptown cab on the way to the museum, waving to passersby or empty alleys. The security guards in the museum are accustomed to someone like Kenny and step forward to dissuade him from making contact; with a little head-fake straight from the basketball court they convince Kenny, who puts his hand back down at his side and hurriedly walks past them. But Kenny cannot be stopped, not for long; Phillip can see that from his vantage point overlooking the foyer through which the small boy now roams.

"Kenny." Philip throws his voice like a dart, stopping the boy in his tracks. He thinks that perhaps it is not the tone but the sound of a voice from nowhere, nowhere that he would expect, that freezes him. "Stay right there, Kenny."

He ducks down a stairway so that if and when Kenny looks up he will not see anyone and perhaps remain amazed and immobile for another five seconds, which he has budgeted as travel time down the hallway and across the Inuit sculpture exhibit, not taking into account the possibility of the security guard's caution for running through the museum.

Kenny is still planted there, looking around for the voice in the vast space of the hall, eyes seeming to swell in his large head as he recognizes Phillip emerging from the crowd.

"Where were you, Bud?" Phillip says and pats Kenny on the shoulder, the contact like a game of tag for Phillip, tension released now that he has found him again and can begin to relax. He checks Kenny to see if he has been in any scrapes in the twenty minutes they have been separated. Scar over the bridge of his nose; old. Chocolate ice cream stain on his windbreaker; newly acquired as of this afternoon. Overall not bad, not bad at all, evidence of a little indulgence. Kenny wipes the dew-drop of saliva from his lower lip, quivering now with what Phillip hopes is excitement.

"I saw colours."

"Yeah, they're pretty, aren't they?"

"Yeah."

"Where did you go, Kenny?"

"To see more colours."

They are linked again. Phillip focuses on the zipper at the base of the windbreaker that he is trying to fasten. Kenny's eyes are fixed on Phillip's downward glance.

"I only have one rule, Kenny. You know that, don't you?"

Kenny, worry entering his face, stares back, as if fearing he has been caught out; there are many rules, but what is the one rule?

"The one rule is that you listen to me when we are out like this. You enjoy the colours, don't you?"

"Yes."

"And you'd like to see more, wouldn't you?"

He nods.

"Well, if your Mom finds out how you've been acting she won't allow us to come out like this."

Phillip then raises his hands as if to gesture *calm down* because Kenny begins to hyperventilate and gives warning of imminent, seismic crying.

"No, no, no. I won't tell her. Don't worry. Not if you promise to be good."

Kenny nods again, folding one hand into the other as if he were trying to make something disappear.

Phillip looks at his watch and suspects that the minute hand may be broken, but that's museum time he thinks, that's Kenny time. Another hour and by then they will be in the cab and once there the day is over really, because Cheryl will be back at the apartment by that time, smiling and waiting for them, not upset at the stain of chocolate ice cream. These things come off in the wash, she would say, kissing Kenny on the forehead and glowing at him.

He and Kenny have this rhythm, he says to himself, as if practicing for Cheryl, this cadence of the day. He gives Kenny the ground rules and then allows him to explore to his heart's desire. He reins him in if there is something that appears to be dangerous, or in this situation, if he becomes rambunctious around priceless works of art.

"You should have been a dad."

"Hasn't been in the cards," he said, doing up the windbreaker that morning as she left for the office to finish up some work for the Alvarez deposition. She was apologetic; it was, after all, unplanned, and she wanted Phillip to know that she didn't see him as the de facto nanny. She trusted him. Phillip replied with magnanimity that it was no problem, that he and Kenny needed to spend more time together, and checked his watch.

The great hall of the museum is full today. Marbled and vaulted, it amplifies whispered asides into a distant tunnelling roar. He feels it now inside his head, a billowing sensation, perhaps because he has slept in this morning; a migraine grumbles near the surface, caressing his left eyeball. Kenny sits beside him on the bench, watching the older kids walk past them and into the sculpture gallery, a squadron of girls laughing about something, not Kenny though, and the indifference is mutual as Kenny is now re-interested in his watch. He takes it off and begins waving it, the strap flapping, now whipping the watch more furiously and giggling with delight.

"Kenny."

Phillip helps the little boy put his watch back on, not an easy task as Kenny wants to help and twists his hand around enough so that the maneuver demands increasing patience and dexterity.

"Don't move your hand, Kenny. That's it, keep it still."

He notices the delicacy of Kenny's hands, how the last two fingers are even smaller, part of the overall picture. He turns the hands over to find the extra crease along the palm that should be there, if what he's read is correct, and there it is. He draws his finger along the fold, the Simian crease, a name out of a zoological museum. Kenny has all the other lines, of course, perhaps not as long or well developed but certainly a fairly normal inventory of loops and markings. To Phillip, Kenny doesn't look like a lot of other kids with Down's syndrome, his eyes are more normally shaped and his mouth opens only when he is tired.

The watch is secured and they sit in silence. Out of the throngs Phillip watches two women emerge: one older and the other in her twenties, a granddaughter likely, given their resemblance. For a moment he thinks that he meets the glance of the younger one, fine-boned and in any other era doomed to be called patrician, but no eye contact is made. The pair continues arm in arm, staring out at nothing, blind planets moving in space. Phillip returns his gaze to the far wall and feels the muscles of his face form an impassive smile.

Phillip prides himself on his inscrutability. It was Delores, only months before she left, who remarked on his lack of emotion as she confided to him the details of her mother's recent surgery (a colostomy revision or bowel obstruction, as he recalled). She was wrong of course, it was less of an exercise in control than sincere indifference—and even then probably not indifference but simply perplexity at being chosen a confident—but he thought about it and concluded that Delores was half-right and perhaps even complimentary: maybe he did have an inner editor, mulling the input and pulling the skin tight on his face. It wasn't that he was insensitive—no, he reasoned, he felt things as deeply as anyone; it was just that his equanimity pleased him. It was the closest to dignity that anyone seemed to allow. That reticence had been most recently road-tested when he first went to pick up Cheryl and was introduced to Kenny without warning. With the boy grabbing him by the fingers and dragging him to see his room, he understood that this was a test, that his facial expressions and body language would be as closely monitored as whether or not their knees touched in the cab ride or the position of her head as they said good-night. He said nothing about it; he was determined to maintain an air of nonchalance, a naturalistic kind-hearted indifference as though she had told him her child had allergies or dyslexia.

"He wants to play opposites with you," Cheryl said as Phillip was plunked down at Kenny's play-table, "you say something and he will say the opposite."

"I don't understand."

"It's a game, he's learning about opposites."

Phil paused, a playful smile deployed for her to see. Sure, he would play.

"The dog runs across the yard."

Kenny stopped, intense effort easing into an answer.

"Two cats sit under the pool," the boy said and clapped his hands, "go, go."

"Then you do the opposite to his sentence," Cheryl prompted, smiling at the two of them. *Christ*, he thought, trying to remind himself of what Kenny had said.

"No birds fly above the desert."

"All bees fall below my dinner."

The child roared with a paroxysmal laughter that frightened Phillip, who rose from the chair with the studied look of a good loser. He smiled at Cheryl and she beamed back.

He could feel her eyes on him all through the meal and it wasn't until dessert arrived that she addressed the topic. What did he think of Kenny? He remembered saying that he thought that he seemed like a good kid. He was going to have to bring it up; not to would mean that he was simply disingenuous, indicating too proficient an actor, no doubt with an eye cast toward the offstage door. He told her that it must be difficult raising him alone, especially with her job at the law firm and then asked if he went to school close by. She smiled.

His head is filling with water. The hydraulic pressure evenly transmitted now along the inner table of his cranium. His eye is especially animated, toggling in its socket with each heartbeat. He reaches into his jacket pocket, promising a goat and a virgin for the first deity that will help him procure a tablet of Tylenol, Fiorinal, butorphanol, anything, but his fingers flutter through the darkness and space finding nothing.

Kenny likes him. Yes, but Kenny likes anything that isn't threatening or comes with a day-glo super ball or a day out. It takes his complete energy to spend the afternoon with Kenny because with Kenny there comes many subsidiary considerations: general appearance upon return, risk of damage (to or by Kenny), and risk of loss. This is the most grievous because all others can be explained by his ward's *Kennyness*. Something shatters or rips and all Cheryl has to do is look at him, and he could be doing anything, laughing, simpering, idling in obliviousness, and she melts; the infraction is forgotten. It is, of course, not as simple between Cheryl and him, he thinks, and more than ever he finds himself reexamining every line of dialogue, cross-referencing their conversations with those of mutual friends and monitoring his gestures to eliminate anything that would make her wary of continuing with him, of talking about moving in and making it official.

It is not the way he imagined it was going to be. Even before he met Delores, Phillip had allowed himself a theoretical family: a boy and a girl with ages beyond infancy or toddlership, avoiding the aching ears but with nothing yet hormonal. They were not faces seen as much as situations: soccer games and other super-8-recorded incremental triumphs. After his divorce he was increasingly less able to conjure domestic scenes and finally, when pressed, could only summon memories of fellow summer campers, vague rumours of bed-wetters and small animal torturers.

He remembered the day the divorce became final, that he wasn't upset or vengeful towards Delores. At the time, he thought that it was a mature response, but in the years that followed he slowly realized that it was just another example of how indifferent he had been to his life slipping away. He had never been an angry man, at least never upset enough to examine, much less change, his circumstances. And so he had a life that progressively disappointed him, lulled him with successive, dull miseries. He drifted from a job writing advertising copy, to something a friend of his set up for him doing technical writing for some internet start-up. Now he taught English to people who had to learn the language to stay in the country and would stare at him with their own vague and persistent hunger. Behind him, he left a trail of addresses of diminishing prominence: second-floor greystone to condo sublet and finally a studio with a midget fridge that he did not bother to stock with beer, as he had vodka in the cupboard. He woke up when he met Cheryl. She saved him and he knew it. He looked around and saw squalor and how far he had fallen and if he did not take control, he told himself, he would eventually wake up to a life he could not change.

And so Kenny and Cheryl would be his family, eventually, or so he hoped. He was spending every weekend with them; sometimes just with Kenny, like this, when Cheryl had a deposition to prepare, and sometimes all three of them, as Kenny did not take being left with his aunt with any sentiment less than a face of rage and betrayal that would haunt Cheryl for the rest of their weekend together. And so he cleaned up Kenny's split lips and took him to the men's washroom when they were all out together and felt through it all that Cheryl was watching and surveying a future that he hoped to share.

A dozen parallel lines appear before him and begin to undulate. The area the lines take up in his visual field slowly expands and now it looks like water dripping down a rock-face, bleeding in towards him. The pressure waves in his head are building and if he doesn't find anything to calm it he'll be spending the cab ride home with his head out the window. He turns to Kenny to convince him to go to the gift-shop where they must obviously sell analgesia and finds the bench empty, its cushion slightly dimpled in the middle.

Phillip stands up. He discovers his head has acquired a gravitational centre of its own, wobbling on his neck as if expressing a desire to separate itself, hop off the shoulders and role into a patch of quiet darkness under a chair. He looks around for Kenny, who cannot run that fast—this is what he has been reduced to: calculating search perimeters like a southern warden with a pack of hounds in tow—and thinks he may hear the voice, the little nasal grunt, in the exhibit of surrealist art, and so he follows. The halls of granite and marble begin to scintillate as though they were aberrantly electrified: a beauty, a travesty, something not up to code. Lines appear like tungsten grills in the centre of his field of vision before they fan out and pulsate. He walks through the central hall where the works would be prominently displayed if he could see them, which he can partially, he thinks; the colours shimmer and disperse and might be the drippings of the surrealists for all he cares.

Cheryl has talked him through this exhibit before; her firm had rented the entire museum for an evening where he was introduced to her law partners and their spouses. It was an outing he attended under the 'expand your horizons' and 'meet her work-associates' clauses of blossoming relationships, a two-for-one that initially pleased him. But it had been a disaster from the start. He tried to hide his irritation when Cheryl took him aside and gave him an impromptu tutorial on the Berlin dadaists, the subtle changes in composition that defined Arp's later works, and Tanguay's use of colour. Cheryl then took off to work the room, satisfied, he thought, that her dullard boyfriend was acceptably briefed. For the rest of the evening he was left to wander among the litigators, hopefully to cough up an insight or two. In a darker moment, one spent smiling into a wine glass and absorbing the nuances of recent changes in the tax code from one of Cheryl's associates, he had fancied a quicker exit: the supernova of an aneurysm for which they could have carted him out with some dignity under a nice quiet death shroud. At times, Phillip bemoans his talent for making conversation because it makes his silences play like a car alarm. Cheryl picked up on it, of course, and was upset and quiet all the way home—thinking, reconsidering, he supposed. He was appalled when he caught a glimpse of himself in the rear-view mirror of the cab that night; did he look like this to her? He saw an expression that he imagined gave away too much, a face like Kenny's, of someone familiar and pitiable.

She told him to let go of her but he did not want to let go. He grabbed her wrist and she told him again, to let go of her. But it was her; she pulled away from him, twisting the wrist and visiting upon it a mark that they used to call an Indian burn but now was just an abrasion. *It was just an abrasion.* She wrapped her hand around her wrist and held them at right angles to each other against her chest and told him to leave, and that's all he could remember of her until she called later that week. What had come over him? she wanted to know. He thought about the sequence of events that had led them to this, all of it choreographic because he could not think of the reasons or remember the word; Kenny was in the next room: there were no words. It was difficult for him to recall the incident at all, and so it took on the feel of a physics problem of many tricky steps. She turned away from him and he did not want her to. He grabbed her wrist because he did not want her to turn away. She turned away because she was finished speaking to him. An extra foot-pound of torque applied—he thought of the situation in its most physical sense, because how did anything else make sense? An extra chromosome and not the lack of love, a spreading depression in his brain, easing him into a migraine, an extra-foot pound and an abrasion. There was no intent in it, he told her, and he felt she believed him, after a time.

Kenny was his saviour. As part of his rehabilitation after the wrist incident, Phillip took him to the Thanksgiving Day parade, fighting the crowd and the oppressive gaiety to place Kenny at curbside as the comic dirigibles floated over them, penitently introducing the boy to the characters that were popular before his time. No, Bullwinkle and Rocky were not brothers, not that he knew of. A large cartoon cat, the one that is forever seeking lasagna, was pulled off course by a gust of wind that had tunneled down the avenue and drifted over them, deflating rapidly: a face absurdly collapsing, a body in the midst of a terrible feline asana. Phillip recoiled and prepared to bolt, thinking the balloon was coming down on top of them but Kenny just stood and squealed approval at the floppy shell.

The world is larger. The people are reduced to cartoon characters and then ants scuttling along the floors of this vast palace. Around him the walls inflate and the little globs of art fold into themselves. He hears the wind, as though emergency doors have been thrown open and the museum has been flooded with sweet, stinging air. In the distance the gift-shop flutters like an oasis. He walks toward the shop, the world swirling slow around him, his arms weightless in the eddy currents. He can hear it all now: every conversation they have had, the point and counter-point, the sound of her breathing as she dreams. He can hear Kenny, who after evading his search now spontaneously materializes at his side in the gift shop, asking for dollyclocks. *Dollyclocks*, he repeats and looks at Phillip as though he were the idiot, because he cannot understand. Is it a toy? Is it a happy meal from one of those movies he is now forced to sit through? What's a dollyclock? he says to Kenny, trying to keep him in his visual field. Kenny points to a bin of remaindered books with torn covers and out-of-date calendars, mouthing the words that Phillip now cannot hear.

He looks toward the desk because that is where the analgesia should be sold but Kenny is on his sleeve, tugging and continuing his chant. I understand, he says, but he cannot understand this little boy with his face and his mysterious needs. In the centre of the scintillations his vision bleaches to a neural grey and Kenny's face is gone, blanked out like an innocent in the gaze of the camera. He locates the boy among the milkiness and colours. He reaches for the windbreaker and pulls.

"Let's go."

He is visited with a magnificent agony: there is blood in each step. It hurts so much that he is giddy, and he laughs at the very thought of frog-marching the little runt out from under the discriminating gaze of the local art doyennes, through the rows of tchotchkes poised only an axe-handle's length from him, away from books that promise culture in the form of coloured pictures. He wonders to what type of provocation the security staff respond most proficiently: it cannot be the caterwauling child, common currency in these halls, nor is it the tantrum or gestures of physical force; these are mere accoutrements of guardianship. It may be the haste with which they leave, suggesting theft of a particularly valuable coffee table book or worse yet, child abduction, but the staff cede passage when they see him because they know that look, the visage of blood and ache.

The little boy bawls in the darkness of the cab with Phillip hunched over beside him, listening to the arteries pound and the city muffling its roar. He feels the sway of the cab as it negotiates traffic. The swelling subsides and he can again open his eyes. Outside his head the world has become quiet, even with the boy sobbing for his dollyclocks. His vision begins to clear and he leans over to Kenny, rubbing the boy's arm and examining the windbreaker with its tear at the shoulder and cursing the sharp edges of cabs and doorways and the like.

Nolan, An Exegesis

I knew him when he was still in school, young enough not to be called solitary or to be called anything at all except Nolan. Young Nolan, that was. Before it all happened to him and then it was just Nolan and his father became the father of Nolan. They lived in a council flat off the Ballymallin Road and he used to be friends with my Des before all of this happened. Then, it was like he didn't need any friends and finally he needed nothing but. But, sure, isn't it always like that?

−Mary Dowd, acquaintance

∼

FOUR HUNDRED AND TWENTY SEVEN STILL PHOTOGRAPHS. (SECOND PHOTO DATED 93/8/3: CASTLEBAR HERALD PG.3; HEADLINE: MEDICAL MYSTERY DRAWS ATTENTION OF SPECIALISTS.) SEVENTY-ONE APPEARANCES ON TELEVISION, INCLUDING THE PANORAMA INTERVIEW; (TOTAL ELAPSED TIME 2 HOURS 48 MINUTES 13 SECONDS COURTESY OF RADIO TELEFIS ÉIREANN/ ITN/ BBC / CNN) LAST PHOTOGRAPHED ON A CLOSED CIRCUIT SECURITY CAMERA 95/7/29 IN A BOOTS PHARMACY, HAMPSTEAD, ENGLAND.

∼

What did I like about it? I don't know. I suppose it was that when he showed it he had to shut up, you know? It's what I imagine you would call a paradox, a trick. He had to show it, but couldn't talk about it; and if he wanted to talk about it, he couldn't show it. I told him that he reminded me of a film, you know? The Invisible Man. But the Eurovision shite, with him swaying in the background and having to stick his tongue out, that was too much. It was probably Mr. Symes doing. They had him playing the tambourine, I suppose that he had to, it *is* a song contest and everything, you can't just stand there with your gob open.

—*Des Dowd, acquaintance*

≈

To speak of Martin in the past tense, I'll have you know, is extremely hurtful to his family. He will come back, I am sure of that, because there is a strength in that family that will bring him back home. There is healing to be done there, but there is also love. As to his refusal to help the archdiocese, we must be guided by conscience but also by duty, and let it be said that the disagreement started there. After our investigation it was felt best to let the matter drop.

—*Rev. R.S. O'Keefe SJ*

≈

Initially I resisted speaking on the matter for reasons of doctor-patient confidentiality. I maintained this silence for as long as I could but there came a time when I had to speak out. We must live in a society that has some common values beyond superstition and fear; that's the reason I came forward and it was also my prime motivation for my book *Speaking of Tongues*.

—*R. Edward Leets, MD, FRCS*
Consultant in Otolaryngology

≈

I thought he was quiet at first. I liked that, the feeling that he was shy and didn't know exactly what to do. He wasn't like the other lads, all talk and the like. I have to say that he struck me as being different, but then it was obvious why he was so bloody quiet, what with the image of Christ across his damned tongue. Oh, you just never know about people. When I saw him on the television news, a clip from the Eurovision last year, I thought, well, he's famous now, more famous, and I had my chance.

–Deirdre Connelly, acquaintance
Following arraignment for Solicitation 95/05/04

~

I find it interesting that nowhere is it recorded what he thought of it, the significance of the image. I suspect that the cardinal asked him and, further, that the answer caused the whole investigation to be abandoned. I doubt that Martin thought that it was God's mark, but if not that, what? Why are you special then, Martin? No one asked that. I like to think I would have if he had ever come back.

–Dr. Sean Phillips, MD, FCRP
Consultant in Psychiatry

~

Well, in Chapter Three, which is somewhat technical but not gratuitously so, I describe the history and clinical features of the condition. A geographic tongue is essentially an inflammatory process, the papillae are affected, usually following a non-specific viral infection, and the raised papillae take on a different appearance than the intervening and unaffected lingual tissue. What is unusual here is not the image that the inflammatory process was interpreted as having, that is entirely beside the point, but the fact that the inflammation lasted so long and in such a consistent configuration. That was really quite unprecedented.

—*R. Edward Leets MD, FRCS*

～

Let the matter drop, is that what the priest said? Are you sure he's a Jesuit? Let me tell you, a Jesuit's likely to learn sign language if only for the pleasure of harassing the occasional deaf-mute. Let the matter drop, that's brilliant. I'll tell you what, the last thing they thought about was whether or not the tongue or the image on the tongue was real. Martin's doubt was what they came to assess, and when they found out he was a smart-ass kid that they couldn't trust, not even after twisting his mother against him, then they declared him not to be authentic. For all the nonsense the others put him through, at least they acknowledged him as a freak.

—*Emma Ryan, journalist,* Castlebar Herald

～

That first photo in the *Herald* showed several young men and woman leaving the regional school following a ceremony and presentation of leaving certificates. Our man is the second from the left, second row, beside a woman identified as Bernadette Leary. The mood is celebratory and he, like the others, poses playfully. Thumbs up, all around. Three cheers! He sticks out his tongue at the moment the flash goes off and the shutter clicks. How long was it out there for everyone to see, taking its first tentative tastes of the world and its promise? A second? Two?

—*Himself*

～

They wouldn't let the poor bastard have a drink or a smoke and they kept the girls away from him too. He only really liked Bernie, anyway. And the girls, that was an odd situation, because half of them wanted to see it and in an odd way I think they found it a turn-on, something sinful and holy all at once, like a towelling-off with the shroud of Turin or something.

–Des Dowd

~

This generally falls under the category of stigmata and revelations and the archdiocese becomes involved to the extent that it designates an investigator and should the investigation have significant merit it becomes a matter for the cardinal. So it is all very regulated, many checks and balances and all of the mysteries, Fatima, Lourdes, they all went through the verification process. In Ireland, outside of the apparition of the Blessed Virgin at Knock, there have been few verifications: a statue of the Blessed Virgin in Navan that cried, stigmata, usually at holy week, etc. We regard them all with equal gravity and with circumspection.

–Rev. R.S. O'Keefe SJ

~

INT. COURTROOM-DAY
The Magistrate's POV, looking down at your man in
the dock.

                    MAGISTRATE
    Answer the question Mr. Nolan.

                      NOLAN
    Actually she misheard me. I asked her if

she'd like to meet a cunning linguist.

General uproar.

MAGISTRATE
Order! We will have order!

CUT TO:

From Revelation *by M. Symes*
©Revelation Films, 1997
All Rights Reserved

∽

It was, as they say in American parlance, a grand slam: an apparition of the face of Christ on some young lad's tongue, a nice looking fellow too, very photogenic other than the fact they always had to have him opened up like a clothes dryer, and then there was the endorsement potential. Everyone was interested, quite naturally. I got a call from his father, who I knew from the weekly local talent show, about the week after it was discovered; and though I don't represent this type of client, I handle mostly musical acts, I agreed because it was just so captivating. There was a possibility for widespread appeal. There was a religious resurgence, and initially, a lot of support from the archdiocese. And then there was the liaison with Mr. Callaghan at the Mayo Development Corporation. If there is one thing I regret, it's the ill will that has come about from all of this. But he made his choice, that's what the archdiocese and his father and Callaghan didn't understand. He grew weary of being manipulated.

–G. Symes, Representative

∽

DISCHARGE SUMMARY
ADMITTED 94/4/21 DISCHARGED 94/5/11

ADMISSION DIAGNOSIS: *Major depressive disorder*
DISCHARGE DIAGNOSIS: *Depression (see below)*

DSM IV

axis I–293.83 *Mood disorder–mixed features, due to medical condition*

axis II–799.9 *deferred;*

axis III–529.1 *geographic tongue*

axis IV–*problems related to primary support group*

FOLSTEIN MINI-MENTAL STATUS EXAM: *27/ 30.*
TOXIC SCREEN: *Amp—neg. Benz—neg. Cocaine—neg.*
MICROBIOLOGY: *VDRL—neg. HIV—neg.*
CT HEAD (WITHOUT CONTRAST): *normal.*
EEG: *non-specific slowing centro-temporal regions bilaterally; EEG (sleep deprived) nil epileptiform, normal background.*

Following failed attempt at self-harm. Secondary stressors include recent relationship failings. Some delusions of grandeur. Responded well to cognitive psychotherapy, initial plan for treatment with SSRI opposed by patient, family. Patient agreed with conservative management and was discharged once it was felt that he represented no harm to self or others. To be followed in the outpatient clinic.

–*Dictated by G. Musgrave for Dr. S. Phillips (not read)*

∽

I only had one problem with Nolan Senior and it was getting that agent involved. From that point on we found ourselves constantly having to submit any plans to Mr. Symes, who, I think it must be said, was not supportive of the idea that Martin's condition should best be used to further the interests of the community.

–*Victor Callaghan, Mayo West Development Corp*

~

Silence. Cold jets in your face and then just relief. But the stink! Hell's own chamberpot. A sniff would have been enough but a mouth full of the Liffey would kill you faster than the drowning. It would erase your visage and his, this baptismal font. Is that what you want? They will ask. A pivotal moment here, celebrated with our own Zapruder film, 8mm, looped and grainy. What would a nadir be without one? Run it backwards as you thrash, your clothes harrowing and thick in the tannery soup, watch the distant siren approach, an ambulance careening in reverse, screeching to a quay-side stop. The men race out, leap backwards to the doors, pull them open and out you come on the stretcher, on which they cart you to the edge. Now there are ropes, a harness around you, lowering you in your wet clothes into the river where you meet yourself, from another film. This swimming is not in sync, you say, and so it isn't because your twin submerges, the water swells and froths and now your errant friend explodes out of the water like a minion of Sea-world, shot into the sky, clothes dried by flight, to gently land feet first and circus-fancy on the O'Connell Street bridge. A look at the river, a look up. Off you go down Dolier to Pearse Street, no one the wiser to your odd gait as they all walk backwards too. And suddenly there you are, on a bench by the green with her. Your very own Jackie O, no funny hat but bits of you all over her. Her words are incomprehensible in this rendition. Your heart does not heal. The image skips, the frame appears, disjointed, shuddering, and everything—the girl, the green lawn of the university, the sky— bubbles and dissolves in the heat of the projection bulb. Back into the water with you! An extra gulp of Liffey piss. In the distance the braying of an ambulance. They've come for you.

—Himself

~

Daily Mirror 94/4/17
Violent Outburst Mars Eurovision Celebration

AMSTERDAM—In the midst of the celebration of an upset victory at the Eurovision Song contest, police were called to restrain the most renowned member of the Irish entry, Martin Nolan, who had become violent and had begun destroying the backstage lounge.

The reasons for the outburst are unclear, although Nolan seemed to become enraged after seeing himself in performance on the monitor. "He has been under a tremendous amount of stress," said Mick Symes, co-performer and son of Mr. Nolan's agent, Gerry Symes.

Dutch police estimate the damage at approximately £2000. No one was injured in the incident although the Italian entry, the folk-singing duo of Anno and Ciaphi was shaken up. Mr. Nolan was detained and then released into the custody of his agent. Princess Diana, in Amsterdam at the time, was not in attendance (See page 3 story: "What's the Stigmata with Martin?")"

∾

My understanding is that they wished to preserve the image on his tongue, and that his various *handlers* forbade him to ingest any chromagen, anything that would discolour the tongue. Tobacco, food, antibiotics, anything could disrupt the image.

–*R. Edward Leets, MD, FRCP*

∾

Why should it happen to him? Why anyone. I wish I knew but these things are mysteries beyond our apprehension. We must be contented by that.

–*Rev. R.S. O'Keefe SJ*

~

I think its wrong to blame the parents for everything. I know that may be considered heretical given my occupation but I would like to say, in their defense, that their son refused therapy and was judged to be competent to do so. He could have chosen to walk away from any of this at any time. His life with the tongue made more intuitive sense to him than without it. It is not a psychiatric disorder to make bad choices. Not yet.

–Sean Phillips, MD, FRCP

~

Castelbar Herald, 93/10/1
Persistent Image Draws Papal Envoy

> Mr. Martin Nolan Jr, age 18, was questioned by a contingent that included Father Robert O'Keefe of the archdiocese and Reverend Cardinal Miguel Auroyo of Santiago, Chile. This was followed by a meeting that included representatives from the Royal College of Physicians of Ireland. No disclosures of the meetings were made public and the participants had no comment.

~

I had an opportunity to discuss the situation with his family, with his mother, really. His parents were recently estranged and she had come from Mayo to see him when he was admitted. His father chose not to make the journey. His mother was a quiet woman. She asked intelligent and appropriate questions about Martin's condition and reenforced the son's wish not to receive pharmacological treatment. She didn't wish to speak to him but had the opportunity to watch him as he slept in his room. As I left the hospital I saw a car from the archdiocese waiting for her, it had been there all afternoon the driver told me, but apparently she wished to walk.

–Sean Phillips, MD, FRCP

～

I'm reminded of those stories where an amateur astronomer, any one of those backyard hobbyists with a store-bought telescope, first sets eyes on a comet or an asteroid or whatever. The comet is always named after them. It's touching, I suppose, to the outside world—a world made up of other novices—but I can't help but think of the serious scientists who have devoted themselves to this pursuit and lived a hermit's life in a mountain observatory. I wonder whether they cry or seethe. Or whether they take to their telescopes to have a look for themselves. Anyway, in my pursuit there were never any real comets. Maybe that's what did me in.

–R.S. O'Keefe, SJ
From the documentary After the Vow *1998*

～

We had in mind a contextual development. It's no use plopping the lad down and having people pass through, it would have been no better than the set-up his father contrived. A plan like that tarnishes the community and casts a bad light on all of us. We proposed something of a higher quality, permanent construction, a site overlooking Clew Bay, good roads, security. The stumbling block was the archdiocese, who still carry considerable weight, even on the commercial zoning board, and of course Martin's father and Mr. Symes. His mother was on the side of the church, or at least expressed her concern for Martin's future in manner identical to the official statement of the archdiocese. All of this can descend into farce, you know, and it has before. There was once a cow, in

County Cork I think it was, who had on her side a patch of brown that was said to resemble the Blessed Virgin; well, they penned it up and renamed it Fatima and even took to selling the milk and promoting its possible medicinal powers. Bloody 2% milk Fatima, they called it in the end. Sad. I didn't want that for Martin.

–*Victor Callaghan, Mayo West Development Corp.*

~

When he told me how he felt about me I wasn't shocked or surprised even. We spoke a lot, until this happened to him. Then, when he told me how he felt, I didn't know what he meant. He said that he needed to be grounded and that I gave him that. That surprised me because he never used words like grounded and I didn't know whether I was to take it as a compliment. I told him no, anyway. My parents thought that it was for the best as I was going to stay at the university. We spoke about it the day it happened. Of course I felt responsible. But I had be honest with him and so I told him no and he made a joke about Jesus but I knew it was because he was hurt, so I didn't mind. I told him no. It was for the best.

–*Bernadette Leary, acquaintance*

~

The importance of the Mayo Geographic Tongue Representation, aside from the obvious patriarchal connotations, is that of an alternate expression. It is perhaps the first time in this society that faith has been represented in a non-traditional physicalized manner (the stigmata of the puncture wound as traditional) much less a sexualized one. This is very important in a cultural sense, for it is the concept of Christ as someone who left footprints, who felt his joints ache as he turned to face his accusers in Gethsemane, a Christ tumescent, who experienced physical sensations other than the agony of death. It is the eros to the established agape (cf Kristeva) and is a new and frightening concept for many people in this society.

–*Kirsten Hall Ph.D.*

From Semiotics and Longing, ©*Samourais Press, New York, 1996*

~

I was appalled. I went unannounced, of course because Nolan Senior threatened to have me barred from ever talking to Martin again. But I went and I was appalled. There was a line stretching out for at least two hundred yards, over a small hill it weaved like it was just another stone wall, and as I progressed through it, past the chip vans and the stalls selling the dashboard mementos, I saw where they were keeping him. It was a caravan, pulled up to the spot by a tractor, you could see the tire marks. Inside there was big Nolan holding court with his cronies. Your man Symes was there with Nolan. In front of them was a sign explaining what was behind the curtains, as though people wouldn't know after marching through the bog what they were there for. It explained it all as something mysterious and awesome, something the church was investigating, and implied that special healing powers had been attributed to just the sight of the tongue. It also asked the pilgrims to give what they could into a black satchel. "Ah, that's the stuff, sure," was what was said as I slid ten quid into the sack, velour on the inside. Ahead of me were two men speaking German, one so thin and sickly that he had to be helped by the other. They were crying. The lighting was subdued, for the mood I imagine, and I stepped behind the curtain to see him sitting there, looking tired and wan, dressed in a white terry-cloth bathrobe, small white Christmas tree lights strung over him. It looked like the bloody tinkers. I stopped and looked at him and was glad he didn't recognize me because I couldn't decide for whom I felt more embarrassed. Then he showed me.

–*Victor Callaghan*

Your love, is a lasting love
Of things not yet begun
These words, like the song of birds
Find their place upon my tongue.

Though these feelings give me life
They will remain unsung
And be more precious for having to
Remain upon my tongue

My tongue, my tongue, that which gives me voice.
My tongue, my tongue, in this I will rejoice.

Only you see the beauty
In what I have become
Know your name is the only word
That dwells upon my tongue

–Lyrics from "My Tongue"
©Revelation Music, Symes and Symes. 1994

~

Can tetracycline do it? Absolutely. It produces a condition known as hairy tongue, a dark, very pronounced discoloration. It is a powerful chromagen. Again, much of this is covered in my book.

–R. Edward Leets, MD, FRCS

~

We had nothing to do with that. It was unauthorized. The souvenirs were of a dubious quality and were not offered by vendors authorized by the archdiocese. Unfortunately, because of the legal proceedings we cannot discuss that incident in further detail.

–Rev. R.S. O'Keefe SJ

~

I met him in London. I hadn't heard from him in more than a year. He went to London because he said it was easier on him there. He wrote to me and asked me to meet him at a specific place and time. I didn't tell my parents, I told them I was visiting my sister. When we met, I could see how he had changed. His eyes were the same but he was nervous, as though someone was about to barge in on us there in the coffee shop. He said he had plans and that he was going to turn his life around. He was going to find a job and make people forget about his tongue. He looked as if he hadn't been sleeping and I asked him if he was all right and he said yeah, and then I asked if he was taking drugs and he said only if oxygen was a drug, and then he laughed and told me he wanted to go back to school and go into computers but felt that it might be difficult, that he was a freak now. I told him that I missed him. He kissed me on the cheek and asked me not to mention our meeting to anyone.

—Bernadette Leary

~

INT. FLAT—LATER THAT DAY

An empty cold-water flat, the windows closed and blinds drawn. A lightbulb hangs by a wire. There is no phone, no radio, no television, only a forlorn cot with a sheet draped over it. The door sits on rusty hinges and must be forced open. The two officers take in the atmosphere. One looks behind the bed, the other opens the door to the bathroom.

OFFICER #1 (O.S.)
Well, he's not in the tub.

OFFICER #2
(Bending down to pick up a piece of paper behind the bed)

Hello, hello. What's this?

OFFICER #1 joins his partner.

OFFICER #2 (cont'd)
A receipt for a prescription.

OFFICER #1
For what? Sleeping pills?

OFFICER #2
Tetracycline. Tetracycline 500mg four times daily.

CUT TO:

INT. PHARMACY—DAY

A grainy close-circuit television image of a man in a hat and glasses, standing in line.

Once at the front of the line, he hands a piece of paper to an unseen person in a kiosk.

The music to "My Tongue" rises.

FADE TO BLACK

From Revelation *by M. Symes*
©Revelation Films, 1997
All Rights Reserved

At First It Feels like Hunger

Elaine's brother Dennis arrives with his girlfriend that Friday evening, the headlights of the car tunneling through a crystal-cold night and stopping near the house at a little past ten. Elaine and her mother have stayed up to meet them, as it's the first time he's brought Sarah home. *Sarah*. Elaine loved the name from the moment Dennis told them about her. In the days leading up to their arrival it was all she could think about; she repeated the name over and over to herself and imagined a woman of intelligence and beauty, a figure sitting alone in a garden, aristocratic features heightened in the evening light.

Elaine presses her head to the window to get a closer look at the car that now sits quiet and dark in the drive, the whole scene obscured by her breath that pulses on the pane in front of her. She wipes the window clean with the heel of her hand and is able to make out a light coming on in the car as a door is opened. The motion of her hand on the window produces a delicate honk that causes her mother to look up from the kitchen table.

"They're here." Elaine says, not taking her eyes off the car.

"Come away from the window." Her mother has prepared a meal of cold cuts and bread for Dennis and Sarah and is now taking the plastic wrap off the food. The house is quiet around them, and feels empty. Elaine's other brother, Frank, is at a hockey game, and her father is elsewhere in the house, likely asleep. The faint drone of a television filters in from another room.

"Come away from the window," her mother repeats.

The second car-door opens. There was no way Elaine could

turn away. She holds her breath and squints at the car. She would remember later how difficult it was for her to make out Sarah at that moment, how unnaturally long that first glimpse took. Shadows and forms move in the tangle of lights from the porch and from a little bulb inside her brother's Toyota. It's a full minute until Elaine can discern Sarah: small-framed, walking behind Dennis, appearing to struggle with an oversized suitcase. When Elaine can no longer follow them from the window, she quickly gets up and prepares herself to meet them as they enter the house. She finds herself standing there, on the landing, facing her mother, who swallows and smiles, a look not of panic but rather of someone resigned to the effort of suppressing panic. They look at each other for a moment and stand in silence, listening to footsteps on the porch.

Elaine sees Sarah through a cloud of condensing air as the door opens. She's beautiful, standing next to Dennis. Elaine's mother fusses over the two, urging them to get in out of the cold and making a great scene about closing the door behind them. Elaine hears a stirring in the other room, the sound of recliner being levered into the upright position. Her father is awake.

They're all introduced by Dennis right there in the hallway, with Sarah—still in her parka, shaking hands and exchanging greetings with Elaine and her mother—like a dignitary stepping off the plane into a new country. Elaine's mother apologizes for not having taken Sarah's parka earlier, and Sarah slips out of the huge jacket in a relaxed enough manner to show that she isn't uncomfortable, but quickly too, as though to show that she appreciates the courtesy she was being shown. Elaine watches Sarah pass her jacket over and thinks that she's never been so impressed by the grace of such a simple and otherwise unimportant gesture. Elaine's father appears now beside them, perplexed and smiling through a face that still wears the oblique upholstered creases of a light sleep in a chair. Sarah steps forward and shakes his hand as though she is determined to sell him a tractor that he doesn't need.

He seems caught off guard and grins as he lets go of her hand, bringing new creases onto his face, now a trellis of lines. Elaine feels short of breath, watching her father stand there seemingly unable to respond.

They are shepherded into the kitchen by Elaine's mother and take seats around the table, where Elaine joins the rest of her family in eating salami and bread and trying not to stare at Sarah.

Polite conversation follows with Dennis helping to ease the tension by genially prompting new topics when silences threaten. Sarah is from Montréal, Dennis says, to which Sarah adds that she comes from Town of Mount Royal, a district in the city. She's finished a graduate degree in history and has come to Winnipeg to study; the subject of her Ph.D. thesis is Louis Riel and the Northwest Rebellion. She has two brothers, one who lives in Ottawa and another still in Montréal. She isn't French but she speaks it—fluently, Dennis adds. In between answers she takes small bites of her bread and sips her tea without milk or sugar. Elaine watches Sarah, studying the way her dark hair falls against her shoulders, the ends curling slightly, watching how she spears a sliced pickle with her fork and how it is eaten in three bites. Never one or two, but three delicate bites. Elaine senses that her mother is watching her and her cheeks burn with the heat of a mindful, almost reproaching gaze. She has been warned by her mother that it was impolite to stare at guests, and on most occasions— her mother's quarterly hosting of the book club or when Frank and his friends passed a beerless and bored Saturday night squatting in their kitchen waiting for a better plan to crystallize—it is never an issue; but with Sarah she is physically unable to look elsewhere.

Earlier in the week Dennis called and warned them on the phone that he and Sarah were only going to stay a couple of days, probably just one, before heading out west for a week of skiing. They had been dating for eight months now, and the family, meaning Elaine's mother and Elaine, really, had begun to wonder out loud why they had not already met her. Dennis maintained that it would have been too soon to bring her out that summer, as they had only just started to see each other, so a couple of days at Christmas would be just have to do. Two days, maybe just one. All this makes Elaine acutely aware of the clock ticking on the wall; within her a small but certain panic is rising: Sarah will soon be gone, and the house will again be emptied of anything exotic or interesting.

The atmosphere around the table—of nervous, semi-concealed fascination—is abruptly broken when the door slams and Frank comes in, hauling a huge bag of hockey equipment. He pauses dumbly at the door, as though he has wandered into the wrong house to find its strange residents at the kitchen table. Frank nods as Sarah is introduced by Dennis. As he turns away, Elaine's mother reminds him to leave his equipment bag in the corridor upstairs. There is no response, although the sound of the bag being dropped onto the floor upstairs is heard by all.

Dennis yawns and strokes the area just under his eyebrows. Elaine understands that this is a signal to them that he is tired and that the evening is nearing an end. The dishes are collected and her mother motions to Elaine that she is expected to help to do some washing before they go to bed, a demand that Elaine accepts stoically, as she refuses to be goaded into making a scene. Her earlier attempts at being a gracious host were rebuffed: the offer to help take the suitcases up the stairs was politely refused; it seemed Dennis could manage. Elaine watches Sarah leave before reaching for the dishtowel.

By the time Elaine finishes the drying, she can hear doors close upstairs, a sound with a finality to it, registering the end of an evening. There is a silence, and then voices muffled. No, she's imagining things. Imagining Sarah and Denis talking. Sarah would sleep in Elaine's room tonight, and Elaine would roll out a sleeping bag on the living room couch. She hears the tap opening in the upstairs washroom, followed by a familiar rattling of the pipes from somewhere in the ceiling above her. Her mother quietly goes about her kitchen-work, putting the uneaten meat into plastic bags and into the fridge and shovelling the half-eaten pieces of bread into a Tupperware container instead of putting them straight into the garbage.

"The bread wasn't that fresh," Elaine says, folding the damp tea-towel on the handle of the stove's door.

"I bought it today. It was fine," her mother replies. The lid on the container *thaups* shut.

Frank comes downstairs, swings open the fridge door and rummages through the cold light doused on the shelves of food, ignored by Elaine and her mother except for her mother's optimistic act of placing a plate on the table. He carries containers and brown paper-wrapped cold cuts back to the table. A second trip for mustard and a glass of milk. Pausing after construction of a formidable sandwich, he looks over at his mother, who sits reading a novel at the table. She was into the Russians now.

Elaine watches the two of them sitting at the table, pretending to tidy up around the kitchen. She is, as her parents would say, a snoop. But the truth was that people—especially people being quiet, without the obscuring haze of adult talk and gesture—fascinate her. This includes her brother, who she usually considered incommunicative rather than given to quiet reflection. Almost as much as Dennis, Frank lived away from them: hockey, school and his room. Three years older and it was to Elaine as though every part of him had changed, dissolving the gentle boy he was when he was just her age to a person who only boarded there. It is, she suspects, what people do when they grow up. Maybe what they need to do to grow up. Share houses. Stay quiet. Have a sandwich. Frank reaches over and touches the front cover of the novel as his mother reads it, gently lifting up the flap to see the title.

"So are we just like every other family or are we different?" Their mother looks up and smiles at Frank's question, all to Elaine's growing incomprehension.

"We can be either," her mother says with an acknowledging

smile. "Sometimes we're both."

"Do you know where the sleeping bag is?" Elaine says, hoping to steer the conversation to something that makes sense to her.

"Hall closet, I think," her mother says.

Elaine looks for the sleeping bag at the back of the closet and finds it buried among the other infrequently used objects clustered in the darkness. A thicket of cross-country ski poles. A single snowshoe. She tugs at the nylon bag several times before it finally gives. When she comes out to the kitchen with the bag Frank has already gone, leaving her mother, reading alone at the table. Elaine has the feeling her mother looks up from her book for a moment when she comes in, but cannot not be sure.

Elaine brushes her teeth in the downstairs washroom and marvels at how such an act can become clumsy and odd; as though tooth brushing wasn't a physical movement but an event that could only properly occur in a specific place. Downstairs, in the washroom with a toilet and a sink so small as to be suitable only for hand-washing, she feels left-handed. She has put too much toothpaste on the brush and feels a stinging sensation at the corners of her mouth that doesn't go away until she's washed the foam completely down the drain. She throws a t-shirt over a pair of sweat pants and washes her mouth out again before leaving.

The kitchen was empty. A light left on over the stove. Her mother was now likely upstairs, still engrossed in the Russians, indulging in that life outside her own. Elaine has occasionally sat in on the reading club, watched her mother steer the discussions and politely reprimand those who had not read the agreed-upon number of chapters and for whom the gathering was just another social event. Elaine avoids not just the discussions but reading the books, and while she tells herself that it just isn't her thing, she is uncertain why she can't be bothered to read. After all, it wasn't as though she lacked opportunity or an example. Her mother has heaps of books. She can always be identified as the one with a novel open in front of her; but it is only recently that Elaine notices this, or rather is annoyed by the familiar sight of her mother reading. Frank calls it her 'sneeze guard', this shield of literature that their mother erects. But what is most bewildering to Elaine is that her mother's constant reading should bother her more than if she watched television or spent an equal amount of time out of the house. Her father didn't seem to mind, or if he did he was too busy with the changes around the farm to pull on another loose thread of potential disharmony.

Even if there are no signs of them fighting—few crossed words passed between them at all—Elaine finds it increasingly hard to understand the secret behind her parents' compatibility. It's implausible to her that her parents ever actually managed to discover each other, much less decided that that discovery was the one on which they would base their future happiness. Elaine knows only the barest details of how they met: her mother, fresh from downtown Estevan, Saskatchewan, adjusting to life away at university—*did her every movement seem strange in the foreign country of a dorm room?*—meets her father at a dance put on by the Agricultural Students Association. Did she have a book that night? Did she put it down to accept his offer to dance, to see him again, to become his wife? How does Elaine's dad present the altered plans to his fiancée when his own father dies the next summer, a hundred head of cattle already keening for the old man? Elaine imagines that he gave her a choice: stay at school, or come with me. She likes to think it was his honesty and straightforwardness that would make him propose like that, that it wasn't meant to be the ultimatum that it sounds like.

So: farm wife instead of teacher. Nothing more said of it. Her mother accepts her new role with the same equanimity as she does Dennis' arrival the following spring or the thinly disguised contempt of her mother-in-law (the last detail a slightly slurred admission told in confidence to Elaine by her Aunt Sylvia after Grandma had died and Sylvia herself had drained the better part of a flask of something to gird herself through the funeral).

Although Elaine doesn't like to think of it, she can't help but imagine that her mother wanted another life, perhaps just the one she was about to embark on when her father stepped in with his proposal. Teaching somewhere; an inner city school or maybe a school overseas, someplace doing volunteer work. Elaine thinks of all the possible lives awaiting to be unfolded in front of her mother at that moment, and how they were closed up so quickly in succession, as though summer had ended and the winds would only become colder. Elaine imagines how such regret could feel, like the dull pain of waiting for a meal, and it scares her to think that they are all a reminder of that regret, and that a book must be held up like a shield to obscure it. That a book can somehow accomplish this.

The sleeping bag smells of basement walls and lack of use, and despite keeping her socks on Elaine is chilled as she straightens her legs into it. The bag is insult enough, but she particularly resents having to sleep in the living room; more than having to leave the comfort of her room, the living room was not designed for sleep: orange tinted lights from outside pour in and light up the ceiling. But it's more than just a night of tossing. She's always the one called upon to move whenever it's necessary, as long as she can remember it's been this way. Sarah was only the latest of a long line of relatives and guests to make her unroll the sleeping bag. She didn't mind it much though, for Sarah, although she would have liked to share her room with her, glad to give her the bed and say goodnight in that way that brings the night to a true end. Instead, she lay staring at the cross-hatched ceiling, waiting. Listening.

Elaine orients herself and imagines the point above her where Dennis' room is and the path he will have to take to get to Sarah. He would wait an hour, maybe longer, until he was sure the house was sleeping, and then a door would open and the sound of footsteps would shift along the hall above her. They would speak to each other in the dark. They would hold each other. Elaine wonders what they would say. She thinks that he must have already told her about the farm, but if he hasn't, that such a moment, there in the dark, would be a suitable time.

Even now, two years after her father finished converting the farm, it was something they all still had difficulty explaining to strangers; and as much as Elaine wanted Sarah to stay a full week, there was a part of her that would have been happy to wave goodbye to her as soon as possible. Outsiders didn't understand, and explaining what type of farm it had become and reasons that demanded the change embarrassed Elaine.

It had been a decision made three summers ago, after her father met with various people at the Credit Union in Brandon and had been given as much of an ultimatum as anyone could receive. There was no longer any money in cattle. The market had collapsed and if he did not come up with a plan, a plan that did not involve simply refinancing their current money-losing operation, foreclosure would ensue. Elaine remembered the grave look that her father wore that winter as he conferred with her mother and her Uncle Steven in Winnipeg. All of the children could sense the tension; even Dennis, who would come home once a month from university, was concerned by the silence at the dinner table.

That autumn, their father's announcement of his decision was met with confusion and consternation. None of them had ever heard of PMU farming and their father, realizing the importance of familial solidarity in the venture, dutifully told them what pregnant mare's urine contained—and how it would save their farm.

It was in this manner, informal lectures around the dinner table, that Elaine and her brothers were introduced to the principles of equine endocrinology. Their father explained that the placenta of the pregnant mare produced great quantities of hormones, of estrogen, specifically, and that this could be collected and used in medicines. The hormone and the urine in which it was found were valuable because the medications they led to were tremendously beneficial. It was a good thing for people, he said, as if trying to convince them that the plan was really a humanitarian effort. Regardless, he continued, it was what they would do. There was silence. They were no longer cattle ranchers. They would collect urine.

The remaining stock was sold off and the barns were brought down or refitted with equipment that none of them had ever seen before. Any objections they had were made secondary to the effort of making it work and saving the farm. While they had always had horses around, now they had to get used to the thought of them as the working livestock, shuffling in their stalls, scooped-shaped collecting devices strapped under each animal, all connected through a system of PVC pipes to a series of forty gallon plastic collecting drums. The drums stood at the near end of each line of stalls, each one a squat totem. Elaine's father busied himself with overseeing the plans and financing and had his hand in every detail of the conversion. The stalls were fitted with a system of black plastic pipes that drained into the nearest collecting drum. The drums were then emptied into a central receptacle at day's end. The system was cleaned nightly, first with water, then with a cleaning solution to stop bacteria from spoiling the hormones in the urine. Then they had to flush out the pipes with water. It was vital that the daily cleaning be coordinated and done quickly, as it was the only time the horses were unhooked from their collection scoops. All members of the family would congregate in the main horse barn and run through the precision-timed maneuvers. *Water flush/ lift scoop/ shake/ acetic acid/ lift scoop/ shake/ water flush/ lift scoop/ shake. Next horse.*

Whenever spillage occurred to a horse they were tending their father would look at them like they were throwing a pocketful of change onto the floor. "One less year at the college for you, Elaine Rose," he said once, before understanding how far that sort of comment went.

As foreign as it seemed, through the months of that first

autumn they all became accustomed to the rituals that a PMU farm demanded. To all the world their father had regained any confidence he may have lost, but in spite of this Elaine noticed that he was quieter now, more prone to just standing in the barn and staring at the horses.

Outside, Elaine hears the barking of one of the dogs. A short burst of three or four guttural shouts followed by silence and then another two that close the outburst like a door slamming shut. She gets up and pads over to the window, staring out into the orange outdoor lights, seeing steam rise from the silhouette of one of their shepherds. The dog stands still in the distance for a moment before another wreath of vapour appears and dissolves around it. Then the animal turns and lopes, head held down, back into its pen, its gait and posture at that moment looking more wolf than dog.

Elaine returns to the bag to find it has gone cold in the minutes she's been away, damp-towel heavy as though it had no memory of human warmth. It seems to her willfully cold and uncomfortable.

When she hears the noise she thinks it's her imagination, the sound of her shivering amplified through the quiet house. Another sound follows, the old bones of the house shifting under the weight of a carefully placed footstep. Had she been upstairs Elaine was sure she could have heard the hinges of Dennis' door whisper. He was awake, on his feet. Moving. The sounds continue, traversing the ceiling above Elaine, periodic and deliberate, moving to where Sarah lay.

There would be intimate words, as soft as the footsteps that brought him. He might tell her he loved her. Or whisper something dirty. It's likely that her parents spoke like this, under the covers, that they, like the rest of the world, conducted their truest business in voices that did not carry. It was all part of that dark mystery forever in another place: words between adults, imagined like now or detected beyond walls or sifting through heating ducts. From her bedroom Elaine could occasionally hear her parents speak as they sat in the kitchen. At these times she listened avidly; the relaxed tone of their adult voices, unaware of surveillance, was as exotic as any topic that could be discussed around a country kitchen table. But when the financial difficulties of the farm deepened Elaine began to strain for the words themselves, wrapped in the gauze of her parents' voices now seeming purposefully, deceptively flat. On their words rested their future. And so it was an odd relief when her father finally told them all what was going to happen.

Elaine imagined that Dennis was talking to Sarah about them, gently assuring her that he wasn't a hillbilly like his folks, that their visit should be thought of as a field trip. He might even joke about PMU farming, talking about the success of the conversion and how his father was a new breed of farmer, all so as to avoid talking about how close they came to losing the farm and what they had to go through to keep it.

Once the decision had been made there came a succession of visitors. Contractors arrived with the plans for a new barn and stall system, within weeks the foundation had been laid and the skeleton of their new lives was erecting itself, armoured in gleaming corrugated metal. Men from the Credit Union came by and stared in silence at the activity, probably despairing for their own futures that rode on such a plan that must have seemed increasingly more ludicrous. Piss. Horse piss.

After most of the construction was complete, a car arrived from the city. Two drug-company people—an older man who clapped her father on the shoulder when they shook hands and a younger woman in a crisp, grey business suit—politely toed their way through the pastureland and nodded as they were shown the set-up. Later, they sat down at the kitchen table, opened their briefcases and delivered volumes of information to her father about the storage of urine and how payment would be made. Elaine watched her mother's attention glance over the man for a moment before settling on the young woman. It was at that time when they were converting the farm that Elaine first became curious about what her mother thought about things, aware that her mother had opinions that did not relate in any way to Elaine or her brothers or father, but were simply private. Now, Elaine wondered what her mother made of the young woman sitting at her table and joking with her husband; what she thought of the flawless hair and make-up, the ease and glamour of a life unburdened by children or farmers or the prospect of collecting horse urine. The briefcase closed, hands were shaken and a shoulder clapped again. Their car was gone.

On the farm, debt, even bad debt, doesn't carry the shame it does in the city. It isn't the same contagious illness, failure wanting quarantine and hushed silences as you creep by the debtor's doorway. In the country, people drop by and commiserate, while still silently searching you or your farm for traces of difference, of what separates your situation from theirs. It's always done with camaraderie, as everyone realizes that the weather or futures options traded in Chicago and Toronto can turn on anybody and bring the auctioneer to the door in no time. On the other hand, changing your farm, selling the stock and veering off into some bizarre biological venture: *that* will get the town talking.

"Piss farmer," Elaine heard as she walked to any empty table in the school cafeteria one afternoon in the October after the conversion. No sooner had the first trickle of urine run through the pipes than word had gotten out. Maybe it was the son of one of the contractors or a neighbour. It didn't matter. People knew. Weeks of suspicious looks and a half-hearted effort at shunning began. For Elaine, it was a good excuse not to attend school dances. A break from the tribal pressures of pretending to want to hang out with boys she didn't like. But what fascinated Elaine was the initial uniformity of shock and disapproval from the community; it was after all, a rural municipality with its share of rumoured or proven drunks, wife-beaters, and miscellaneous broken homes: none of which provoked anywhere near a comparable solidarity of indignation. She was also surprised at how defiant it all made her feel. It girded her. *Well, we're piss farmers then,* she thought. They were pioneers and would face the same hostility as the first farmer to use a combine or a mechanical milker, the same snickering, dumb faces pleased as punch to be outraged at something.

Dr. Saunders arrived a day or two after the livestock to inspect the operation and the horses. As was his habit, he stopped in to see Elaine's mother first for a chat and a cup of coffee prior to heading to the barn and making sense of their new endeavour. Saunders had been firmly against the conversion, and had told Elaine's father to his face. He said that there wouldn't be much of a future in animal estrogens, that plant and synthetic estrogens would arrive in ten years and make an operation like this obsolete. He also said that he had heard of barns in the States that had made similar conversions only to face protests from animal rights groups, the usual circus of picket signs and threats. Even, a couple of barns had been burned to the ground. Elaine's father, stung by the openly expressed misgivings of a man whose competence and opinion he trusted completely, said that if city people had the same concern about his farm going under and his family not eating, he could take them a little more seriously. Elaine remembered him adding that having a conscience was like using horse shit for manure, if it wasn't applied evenly, then it was just horse shit.

After saying his piece, Elaine's father waved his hand as if to dispel the angry words that seemed to fill the space between them. He paused for a moment and then as though acknowledging Saunders' reservations and wanting to show him he that he had thought about these issues too, told him about their plan to raise the foals and house them in the existing barn. *Would that please the city people?* Saunders was silent, which frustrated Elaine's father even more. *Are you still gonna be my vet on this thing?* he asked, to which Saunders nodded that he was.

Whatever reservations they had about the financial wisdom of such a move were soon forgotten; in the first two years they had turned the farm around, erasing any residual debt and for the first time in anyone's memory, putting money in the bank. But failure would have been easier on all of them. Their plan could have been dismissed as an act of desperation, an exotic pre-bankruptcy flame-out. As it was, they were seen as visionaries, advocating an overthrow of the known and respectable. They couldn't have drawn more attention, or less initial support, had they set their own barn on fire.

The PMU operation became so successful that other cattlemen in the area who had been having trouble soon began to visit their farm, just to see their father's set-up and ask a few questions. The tours were conducted at dusk, the questions posed in hushed tones. Elaine would see the pickups leave as she cleaned out the stalls. Once, a van-load of Hutterites stopped by, the children staying in the vehicle and staring out like alarmed astronauts as Elaine's father took some of their men inside the barn to show them what he had done. A second operation opened on an adjoining farm a year later, and her father had played a role in helping to organize it. There was no need to be competitive, he said, there was more than enough horse pee for everyone.

And now they had foals. Everywhere there were horses. The most sensitive part of the discussions about the farm had been what they would do with the foals. Her father described what was done on other farms; foals were often sacrificed at birth, since raising them to a stage where they could be sold and transported was another cost, in feeding and shelter, that could eat up whatever margin they hoped for. But seeing his children squirming in their seats at the idea, he soon realized that this would have inflated a difficult situation with emotion and recrimination; it would split them at a time when their support was most needed. Her father recognized the pragmatism in the act, and so it was an expense they would have to absorb.

Elaine saw Dr. Saunders often that first summer as he visited the farm to oversee the inseminations and check on the health of their inaugural group of mares. She had always had the habit of accompanying him during his visits, which he encouraged as he found her company enjoyable and felt the girl disposed to intelligently discussing the health of the animals. The summer that they converted the farm he offered Elaine the chance to come on calls with him, and so it was that they founded their friendship, on the weekends, traveling the highways and rural roads of the Assiniboine Valley. He would introduce Elaine as his assistant and she would shake the hand of the stoic, perplexed farmer as she carried the examination gear from the truck to where the problem lay. She asked Saunders questions about the illnesses that certain species were prone to, why pigs seemed to all get sick at the same time, and whether animals could think, to which he replied that he felt animals were capable of a considerable, although not quite human, intelligence. When Elaine asked him what he meant by this he told her that he wasn't certain himself, that it was just a feeling he had.

There were times when Elaine felt it too. Not intelligence, not like Saunders had explained it, but she had felt the consciousness of animals around her. She would stand up to take a break from mucking out the stalls and find the horses' silent gaze on her. Neither she nor the animals were used to them being stalled for so long and Elaine felt a grievance in the eyes of the horses. Saunders nodded when she told him this—she suspected that he quietly shared the horse's complaint.

After a few weeks with Dr. Saunders, Elaine had already seen and helped in most of the routine tasks that made up a country vet's day. She picked up the details of the job quickly and knew how to handle Saunders, respectful of the silences in the truck on their way to calls and knowing what was expected of her when time for the consulting came.

She had learned to set up the intravenous for administering euthanasia, getting the solution ready as Saunders explained the inevitable to the farmer. She would assist him in minor surgery or with treatments, handing him instruments and taking an occasional thrill in being able to anticipate the tool that he would need next. And Saunders would do the same for her: stepping in to steady Elaine, thinking that she was going to faint as they circled around to inspect a laceration and caught sight of the deep sirloined gash on one of Mel Purvis' dairy cows. She kept her feet, and was proud of it, but admitted that she uttered a minor curse at the sight of the wound where a rail had torn open the flank of the incredibly oblivious animal. Saunders sensed it though: not just her alarm but the stiff necked pride at trying not to show it. She thought he appreciated the effort.

"You know cows Elaine, you know how they get in scrapes," he said, bracing his shoulder and head against the cow's flank to steady it for suturing.

"Yeah."

"She's okay."

"Yeah."

The cow made a shuddering movement, as though merely irritated at the efforts to close the wound. Saunders was down to the last skin sutures and waved Elaine closer. He held up the curved suturing needle for her to take and motioned that he was going to step in front of the animal to keep it still.

"Okay now, grab aholt."

The truth is that Elaine had come to forget most everything about cows in the two years since they sold off the herd. She felt ashamed that it could all fade on her so quickly, so easily replaced by different animals and another way of life that until recently had seemed like such a *scheme*. But on visits with Saunders the cows came back to her: the slow grinding and gulleting of feed, the smell climbing up into her nostrils, steeping her clothes, the big-eyed docility that let you sew up a gash without anesthetic. She didn't tell Saunders but she didn't miss the cows a bit.

In the time that Elaine spent with Saunders she observed how quietly he went about the routine of his work and wondered why, although there was never a time that she had not known him, she was not aware of more of the details of his personal life. Saunders lived alone in a two-storey brick house by the water treatment plant near town and was a public figure as visible as the bank manager or the mayor and yet was a mystery that people seemed satisfied to allow to remain unsolved. Nothing personal was given away by Saunders. She knew his name was Phillip: an intimacy not allowed by him but gleaned by Elaine from his University of Saskatchewan diploma that hung on the office wall above the filing cabinets. From the dates on the diploma he was plausibly five to ten years younger than her father. Elaine assumed he wasn't local, as she had never experienced a local who didn't have an acknowledged public history that accompanied them like a shadow. She didn't know where he was born or if he had had any family. In the house where he had his office she saw no traces of the paths of other people. At one time Elaine imagined an estranged wife or even children, all of them victims of an insoluble domestic drama, making the best of it by living in another city. The sadness of a broken home would have been more than made up for by the knowledge that Saunders was at least capable of one great romantic, if sadly doomed, love. But there was no proof of any other person in Saunders' life, not the photo of a parent or a sibling, no snapshots from anyplace she didn't already recognize.

In the time they spent in the clinic between calls, she would take the opportunity to look through his textbooks, trying to memorize the names of the instruments or the technical terms for procedures that were so much a part of his daily speech. In the section of his library on horses she ran across a book on equine obstetrics and found herself unable to put it down. Had she had the nerve she would have asked his permission to bring the book home just to study the illustrations in the quiet of her bedroom. What had all her life seemed natural was now shown as a process fraught with peril at every step. The mechanics of muscles contracting, the physics of moving a large animal through a larger animal, that leap into light and oxygen and gravity. It was wonderful and it frightened her; it made her think of all the things that could go wrong, made her fearful of having children herself. From then on when she looked at the mares in the barn after that she tried not to imagine the buzzing sound from inside them, the terrible industry of life.

In the weeks after starting as Saunders' assistant, Elaine began to daydream about him, imagining what it would be like to have him as her father. Perhaps it was the timing: she had started spending time with him just as her father had sold off all the cows and seemed preoccupied with the beginnings of their new venture. Or it could have been the vacuum of family in Saunders' life into which she was drawn. But despite being uncomfortable at the thought—for lack of loyalty to her father, or, for that matter, to herself—it became clear to Elaine that Saunders and her mother were each the solitary sort of person who would have been ideally suited to each other. She could not stop the images of them together from assembling in her thoughts. Her mother would read his journals and tell him about what looked to her untrained eye to be the big advances; he would help her through her correspondence courses. There might be travel for both of them and more than just the company of a novel for her mother. The thought of all this, and that the two of them might be thinking it too, not acting on it but acknowledging it like some sort of secret, depressed Elaine. She wondered what Saunders and her mother talked about when he went into the house before coming to the barn on a call. He was always professional on calls when she went with him, never a word that could be misconstrued, never joking with the farm women. But things were often said out of earshot. Bigger secrets had been kept.

Her mother and Saunders, perfectly happy together. A world that got along quite nicely without her. It was while in these thoughts that increments of sleep settled on Elaine, obscuring the waking world, draining light. Her sleep was shallow and later when she recalled the night she could not remember having dreamt. If there had been other noises above her, she hadn't been aware of them.

Elaine awakens to the sound of her father putting on his boots at the front door. She hears a boot slap and a groan. He's hurrying. He looks up from his bootlaces to Elaine who has stumbled off the couch with the sleeping bag gathered around her shoulders like a poncho. The weather has changed overnight: snow is squalling and when her father opens the door ice crystals and cold air sweep inside.

"Some foals are gone. Did you lock up?"

"Yeah," Elaine mumbles, the haze of sleep tamping down the word until it sounds to her own ear uncertain or evasive. She rubs her eyes and squints, as if to convince her father that she has just woken up.

"Mom's in the barn so get Frank or Dennis," he says. Standing in the door, he is a silhouette bitten at the edges by the whiteness of the outside: "Get in the truck and go along the eastern trunk road. I'll go up the western fence."

Elaine dresses and goes upstairs looking for Frank. When she finds his bed empty she looks for his hockey bag and finding that missing as well, remembers that he is at the rink. From her room she hears Dennis' voice, constrained and deliberate, making some sort of point that requires more force than a whisper. She pauses in the hallway, hoping to hear Sarah's voice, laughing back at him, and defusing the situation. She hears nothing and waits outside the room before speaking.

"Dennis?"

A longer pause follows. The door opens and Dennis pokes his head out. A ridiculous smile is stretched over his face that makes him ugly to Elaine.

"Dad said a few foals are gone. Could you drive me along the eastern trunk road to look for them?"

"But we're getting ready to go." Dennis says, looking back into the room as though mustering support. Elaine peers into the room and sees Sarah sitting on her bed, face flushed. Elaine wants to take a step back, but doesn't.

"Dad's out already but we can take the truck."

"We really have to get going. It's already past eight."

Sarah stands up. She shakes her head and says calmly, "Christ, Dennis, we can help. It's your family."

Elaine thinks she is going to vomit during the drive to the eastern trunk road. She's closest to the passenger door, wedged in with Dennis and Sarah. The road is difficult to follow in the blowing snow and Dennis curses as he shifts the pickup, steering the truck with a series of dramatic corrections. The rest is silence, just the mysterious, palpable threat that adults—even Sarah—possess.

Elaine opens her window enough to let in pulses of cold air and snow. Under any other circumstance she would be preoccupied by her embarrassment about the state of the old truck, its ragged bench seat, its gun-rack along the rear window that seems straight out of a skit about cousins marrying each other. She has called Dr. Saunders' office before they left, but got his machine and hung up. Even now she could not think of what she would have said had he answered, but nonetheless would have wanted to know that he was there, maybe wanted him to know where she was going.

An area of a mile or two along the eastern trunk road was where they typically found strays, seeking shelter in a poplar grove close to the end fence. She had been out this way before when they had cattle, found several head scratching their rumps on the endposts that marked the limits of their property.

Dennis now seems invigorated, deputized by the weather storming around him. He grunts a little as he jerks the steering wheel to keep out of the ditch. Once the truck has been reined in, he accelerates, pushing them down the tumbling white, obscured road. Sarah says nothing, arms folded across her chest. Holding herself still, containing herself, Elaine thinks. From this view of

Sarah, Elaine turns and stares straight ahead into a thousand collisions of snow against windshield, not reassured by the periodic calm of the wiper blade's wake.

There isn't even a gasp among them when they hit the horse. Elaine thinks she sees a flash of the animal—an apparition of colour, indistinct as a brown blanket being flung at them—lasting a second before disappearing into the blizzard again. What she recalls is the sound of metal dimpling in, a hollow thudding of something absorbing force. A noise repeating itself in her head as though to convince her of its occurrence. Dennis two-foots the brake pedal, leaning the two passengers forward, so they must brace themselves on the dashboard. As the truck stops Sarah puts her hands to her face but says nothing. Elaine can hear Sarah breathing deeply, thinking it is a sound moving towards a sob, and feels breathless on the seat beside the woman.

Elaine pulls back the handle and elbows the door open. Outside the cab, she's immersed in weather, wind and snow slapping against the exposed skin of her neck. She shivers in relief; the cold shaking sense into her, telling her that she's on her own two feet and freed from the cab where Dennis and Sarah still sit in silence. Sarah looks stricken to Elaine, still upset but now past crying. Standing there, with the door open and not a word among them, Elaine is surprised not to feel sad as well, surprised that she can watch Sarah and regard it all as an observation without feeling the sorrow herself.

She waits for Dennis to do something, to reach back and take a rifle from the gun rack, but he sits motionless. She can't remember thinking about anything as she reaches over him. There is only the feeling of standing on the roadside with the weight of the rifle in her left hand. She opens the glove compartment of the truck and takes the box of shells.

"Elaine, stay in the car," she hears Dennis say as she closes the door.

She can see where the foal lays in the ditch. Off to the side she can make out a series of elliptical bites taken out of the snow by a hoof or a head as the animal cartwheeled down the incline. The position of the animal and the distance it lies from the road tell her all she needs to know. Elaine applies pressure to the butt of the shotgun with her underarm. The sound and feel the gun dislocating into its two-hinged component parts satisfies her, makes her think of an elbow flexing to apply itself.

The barrel of the shotgun abruptly swings down and its metal edge catches her right shin. She winces, less at the pain than at how her haste has led to a breach of gun safety. *Complete control of the firearm*, she repeats to herself as blandly as any Catechism, *is the foundation of safe operation.*

Elaine looks through the truck's window while she takes a couple of shells out of the case. She trembles, feeling her heart shouting out in her chest, announcing itself to her arms, hands, useless fingers. But her hand imposes itself on the mutiny, steadies and guides a shell into the gun barrel. Its twin is dropped into her pocket.

She turns and with each step down the ditch the snow becomes deeper, demanding a progressively longer moment for adjusting her balance before she can extricate her trailing foot. The shotgun is another variable, carried in her right hand, held higher than she would normally carry it because of the snow and the loaded chamber. Elaine gives herself one of her father's headshakes at not deciding to load the gun at the bottom of the gully. Halfway down the ditch she understands the full weight of this effort, the energy required to suppress every kind of fear. She feels the desperation of wanting to cry only marginally less than wanting to be free of tears. The difference between the two the thinnest of margins, a small air bubble under the overturned world into which she can lift her mouth to breathe. Up to her thighs in snow, she sees the animal as though she were already above it, nostrils funneling in last breaths, eyes filling with what she can see but cannot understand. That animal pain. She can already anticipate the kick of the shotgun against her shoulder, its echo abbreviated by the squalling snow. Under her a sudden crimson star. All of this is clear and not for a moment coloured with sadness or fear or anger, Elaine realizes, as she reaches the animal to find it already dead.

Generator

---

*Introductory Comments on the Occasion of the Festschrift
for Marcus Epsum, Delivered by Aurora Hearne,
Convocation Hall, West Rye, New York, July 21*

Madame Chancellor and Mr. Symes, honored members of the faculty, invited guests, and finally, Nathalie, David and Patricia.

I would first of all like to thank the organizing committee for their efforts in creating this conference in Marcus' honour and for inviting me to present a paper as well as give this opening address. I stand before you today as a person deeply affected by my relationship with Marcus Epsum. I am only one of many so influenced, many of whom are renowned, others you will never know. It is a privilege, sad and special, to be called upon to gather my recollections into this talk, to try and achieve something befitting the man. I suspect I will fail but am consoled that it may be more a measure of the man's accomplishments than my lack of eloquence.

Marcus began his career as a linguist, with an interest in algorithmic formations of language, specifically macro-syntactitcal structures, that eventually led him into the emerging field of machine translation. With the full bloom of the digital age, unprecedented reductions in communication time were still largely negated by translation problems, as though one enzyme step, one synapse, was fouling the potential of this wonderful system. Marcus wanted to bridge that gap. He spent three years in Strasbourg as a consultant to the European Parliament, trying to develop fully automated high quality translation, which, after years of stuttering starts and diplomatic crises (an untranslated 'put a' became 'puta' with alarming frequency) was dubbed by its acronym FAHQT. He would joke that although their system was FAHQT, it was never nearly as FAHQT as it needed to be. He laughed at his own jokes and made many enemies and friends among the French.

During his time in Strasbourg, Marcus was a solitary figure, using whatever time he had to spare to travel across the border into Luxemburg or into southern Germany. He kept in touch with friends back home, became a fan of what is known here as soccer and wrote poetry, something he had done since he was a young man and which, as young men tend to do, he kept to himself. Over the course of his first year abroad he had fallen in love with a computer engineer named Nathalie Brossard, whom he met at a conference on Idiomatic Mistextualization. Nathalie did not speak English, and at that time Marcus spoke only a rudimentary and poorly pronounced French, and so when Marcus wanted to share his feelings with Nathalie, he turned to the machine that he believed would more accurately deliver his most deeply held thoughts. Legend has it that he translated a sonnet he wrote for Nathalie from English into French using machine translation. He checked the phrasing closely, going back and forth between the English and French versions and when he was satisfied he printed his copy and delivered it to his girlfriend. Nathalie was deeply moved and Marcus understood her pleasure to be simply her pleasure with him, for being a man sensitive enough to try to express his love for her, however modestly. He was very much surprised when Nathalie submitted his poem to a literary journal and it was accepted for publication.

One night, shortly after the poem had been published, Nathalie was getting ready for bed and took the opportunity to leaf through the journal that held his poem. She marveled at the beauty of the poem, especially coming from a man who (and she said this with as much diplomacy as one would expect from an EU consultant) lacked such poetry in his spoken French. She asked Marcus how he came up with such imagery, reading out the lines that had so captivated her, and he admitted (secure in the knowledge that they were safely married and beyond the teeth of certain forms of critical discourse) that he could not remember having written that line, at least not in English, and that particular poetic effect, while admittedly admirable, was not deliberate. But it was written in French, Nathalie said, it had meaning in French. This moment, with the two of them looking at each other in their Strasbourg bedroom, considering what the poem meant and what it had become, is a moment of revelation in narrative, the next in that long line of innovations, technical and textual, from Gutenburg to Joyce.

Marcus and Nathalie realized that what he had done when checking the poem was to inadvertently subject it to repeated English-to-French and French-to-English translations. The first translation had two semantic mistranslations (fairly normal for machine translation at the time); by the seventh translation, there were numerous syntactic and semantic mistranslations, cryptic and haunting. She read the poem again to him and he was amazed and embarrassed; he had created something quite beautiful. They spent that night at the computer, subjecting simple phrases to repeated circular translations.

Marcus typed the phrase, " My head is full of unusual ideas" into the program and translated it into the German and back to English. He repeated the iteration four times until the phrase read "My dismantling text is full of singular thought."

They could not sleep the rest of the night, putting phrase after phrase through the same process until they came up with altered translations, with new meanings. It was not long before Marcus began experimenting with different iterative schema, three iterations of French, then one each to German and Portuguese and back, alternating iterations from Spanish to Italian, three times before bringing it back to English. Marcus found this was the best for approximating verse (an iteration through German near the end produced a nearly-irreparable alteration of metre). He would indicate the number of repeated translations using multiplication signs until it dawned on him that the semantic alterations produced geometrically disparate meanings, and it was at this point he decided on using mathematical phrasings and superscripts in his recipes, and an algebra was born. He initially tested the algorithms on readers—one can imagine gymnasia of extra-credit-seeking freshmen scowling through the results as they were asked to rate each effort for comprehensibility and aesthetic pleasure evoked. And soon, a free-verse algorithm was devised:

$$([English\text{-}French]^3\ English\ Italian\ [Estonian\ Spanish]^2$$
$$([German\ French]\ English)\ [Italian\ German]\ English^2),$$

A Haiku algorithm followed:

$$([English\text{-}Sanskrit\text{-}Serbo\text{-}Croatian]^2\ English).$$

Certain forms of communication—screenplay, automated/ menu-formatted telephone message—could not be made to yield alternate connotative meaning despite rigorous application of all available algorithms. Marcus surmised that these forms of expression had already been passed through the extensive parsing processes of Hollywood and Madison Avenue that rendered them immune to further textual manipulation.

Such discovery changed their lives. Marcus never returned to work at the European Parliament, a decision as easily understood and forgiven as Gregor Mendel's absence at vespers. There was work to do, new work, with results, species of things never before seen that needed descriptions and classification. Let it not be said that he toiled in isolation; throughout all of this Nathalie was a guiding force, and indispensable partner, programming algorithms for rapid application and prose generation.

How Nathalie and Marcus transformed the literary world, how they maintained an output unmatched in the history of modern composition and how they polarized the world of letters, will not be discussed in this forum. Let us just say that we are heirs to that legacy.

And while Marcus' stochastic poetry and prose was finding an increasingly wider audience—something he regarded as victories in the skirmishes of a guerilla war, an insurgency against traditional narrative—his presentation of this linguistic and narrative theory was initially met with skepticism and indifference. His impromptu *Habilitationsschrift*: 'Idiomatic Translation and the Genesis of Narrative Meaning' (including examples run through a devilish algorithm of High German, Yiddish, and Estonian), was summarily (and ironically) rejected by the University of Frankfurt as 'not only meaningless but infuriatingly frivolous'. In a gesture of typical Epsum creativity, he took the text of this rejection notice sent to him by the rectors of the university and, after subjecting it to iterative retranslation, published it as perhaps his most famous prose poem, *Teutonic Penumbra*.

When Marcus returned to the United States, accepting a position at the Dupont Institute of Advanced Study as the first Chair in the Department of Stochastic Linguistics, he arrived with a singular purpose in mind: to apply his program to all existing text. It was an ambitious project, one that required a parsing system until then not yet imagined but one that he and Nathalie were successful in developing, a new narrative engine that they christened the Stochastic Iterative Narrative Generator or SING. He knew that the power of the process lay in the limitations of Machine Translation, that the errors of semantics and syntax, the stochastics of the process, would amplify into new meaning, something we had not seen before. When asked if this was Benjamin's concept of a meta-language coming to fruition, he only smiled and said that where Benjamin wanted to find the language between the language, he wanted to find the language outside of the language.

It was when he was in the midst of the initial application of the SING that I met him. As I have admitted in my own work, I was initially contemptuous of everything SING stood for and felt that Marcus and Nathalie's work was an affront to narrative, to the process of creation that we as living, sentient beings, hold dear as our gift, our responsibility. My view of the process, and by extension, the man, was dim, if not damning, as he was taking a complicated, nuanced cerebral process and had superficially succeeded in having it reduced to the equivalent of an ATM transaction.

It was in my months of working under Marcus' tutelage that this animosity dissipated. I was overcome, in increments, by the unending stream of beautiful words that emerged from the process. Whereas I had always thought that the development of each algorithm was simply a matter of Marcus' caprice, I discovered that it involved an 'evaluative process' where volunteer readers scored random passages in terms of lyric beauty. Can you imagine that? I thought, taste-testing words like they were tooth-picked Vienna sausages. But that is what Marcus said validated the process. It didn't take long for the A.I. people to approach Marcus with their proposal for a neural net—they couldn't resist being a part of a project that they joked elevated a Turing test to the level of art. Like the rest of the world I was left speechless by the groundbreaking *Argot Project*, to which I am proud to say I made a significant contribution . (Pause for applause) Anyone, including me, who viewed the output of the man, was eventually left without counterargument. I have had a difficult time coming to terms with it, as I have detailed in my own writings. My conversion to an advocate of SINGing was met with consternation and, later, repudiation in other critical theory circles. I was seen as a betrayer of my cause, and, in what is the worst criticism that can be leveled against an academic, as a person easily swayed. Arguments raged: Jauss and Barthes, in their seminal papers on Epsum's work, betrayed their modernist biases in saying that the changes in the readers' expectations were the true value of the process and proposed that such texts were invalid if unaccompanied by all the translations. What they misunderstood, of course, was that the algorithms that generated the words had been vetted by readers. Those who didn't understand said that Marcus thought the reader was insignificant, but the reader was central.

And that is perhaps the highest compliment that can be paid to Marcus. The reader was central.

Of course I don't want to discuss recent events. They are a wound which must be given time to heal. It is no secret that Marcus inspired an unprecedented depth of emotion. Many were devoted to him, others to the dream of destroying him. I understood that well. That's why when I heard the news of this madman, this disgruntled *fan*, I was not surprised. I could almost hear the gunshots ring out across the country, as I could nearly feel the impact. At one time, forgive me, I understood how someone could have reveled in the imagined kick of that pistol. We have no words for such things, no iterations suffice.

Marcus Epsum wanted technology to generate beauty, and if it created a different meaning, even a lesser meaning, it could still be valued by someone who took the time to read it, to instill it into the next, necessary act of generation. As Marcus said, with a little help, 'My dismantling text is full of singular thought.'

Thank you.

The Death of St. Clare

Throughout the summer of the year I lived in Washington, I spent much of my time at the National Gallery of Art. As much as the museum was a place for visual stimulation, I have to admit that I was first attracted to it by the sounds. I would linger in the galleries for hours, floating through the space of the foyers like a giant satellite, picking up and registering the heartbeats of those around me. I circled the world and recorded everything: weight shifting from limb to limb, coughs, whispered appreciations. The silences, too, were exquisite, broken only by footsteps that crackled through the marbled halls like distant gunshots. I listened to my own feet and their echoes.

My tastes were forming, and like any young man alone in a new city I found myself drawn to work that showed the loneliness I imagined I felt: Hopper's empty streets, the impenetrable walls of colour on every Rothko canvas. In West Main Floor Gallery 35A, I stopped at a painting that I had seen before but only in passing. The gallery, which contained 15th and 16th century religious paintings from Germany and Austria, had not up to that point made any impression on me. Strigel's *Saint Mary Cleophas and Her Family* hung across from Koerbecke's *The Ascension*. In the far corner Reimenschneider's *A Bishop Saint* glowered. All of the paintings were austere and medieval-looking, not my taste at that time, but for some reason that day I hesitated in front of *The Death of St. Clare* by the Master of Heiligenkreuz.

The Death of St. Clare is a death bed scene, and in that sense the painting was nothing out of the ordinary for this gallery, where every work warns that disease and plague are common, that birth and death share the same bed. St. Clare, the abbess of the order, is breathing her last and is surrounded by nine other women. The Virgin Mary supports her head and at her side four virgin martyrs stand with haloes blossoming behind them. In front of the bed, two fellow sisters of St. Clare sit, each studying a book that lies open on her lap. Another sister stands behind the head of the bed, eyes averted from her dying patroness to the book she is holding. First I looked at the faces for a long time. Those elongated foreheads and the inhumanly long fingers reminded me that the Renaissance was still heading northward when The Master committed this to canvas. I studied the painting for a little more than an hour that day and went home, but I spent the night in discomfort and slept poorly.

The next day I went to the gallery's curatorial library and began to read everything known about the painting. Inspired by a vision of Sister Beneventura of Diambra, it had a rather simple provenance, only ever having been exhibited at the NGA and Munich's Alte Pinakothek, where it hung in the mid-nineteen-twenties and was likely appreciated by any number of former art students. I also learned about the woman: that St. Clare's legacy was the establishment of her religious order under the Franciscans, approved by the Pope two days before her death, and that she had been confined to bed by a mysterious illness for thirty years before this final scene was played out. This gave rise to her latter-day notoriety: the chronically ill and bed-bound Clare prayed to be able to see mass and a vision of the celebration appeared, miraculously projected on the wall of her bedroom. In 1958, just days before his death, Pius XII declared her the patron saint of television.

The next day I returned to the museum and I found myself drawn to Gallery 35A where I took my place in front of *The Death of St. Clare*, watching. I examined the eyes that day—huge and sad, looking into themselves. Looking at the painting relaxed me. I felt that things had a special meaning for me at that moment and wondered if anyone else in the gallery could understand this or could feel it too. I saw myself looking in, saw his gaze fix itself intently on my face, on my hands arrayed on my chest like a bouquet.

I had difficulty sleeping after that. I rolled around in my bed for six or seven hours every night and then I would get up and think about going to the Gallery again, returning to the painting. It was early fall and my constant presence did not attract much attention. The museum is full of people like me. You think we are moving around, but sit down and watch us. We don't circulate. We find our spot and we hover like hummingbirds around the mouth of a flower. One day, while paying particular attention to the angels that floated above the head of St. Clare, watching the thuribles arc through the air and taking in the aroma of the mountain air that sifts through the abbey, I first experienced that sense of connection. I had found my place.

This is not to say that I slept better, I didn't; but who could sleep with the scene set out before me? By day I held vigil at that bedside, sitting with the others and watching her cheeks tremble with each breath. There was a tightness in my throat as I watched St. Clare. I felt as though the world around me was dissolving, the colours miscible and the shapes shifting, breathing. I would emerge from the building every evening moments before the museum closed its doors, as though I had just awoken from the most fantastic dream, something inexplicably full of meaning, and would find myself in the twilight of a city, a place that had no name because names had ceased for me. At the same time I felt that I had become nothing, that the eyes of St. Clare were more substantial than the person standing before them. It was a bleak thought and one that frightened me for a moment. But there was no cause for surrender, only realization.

I am these imploring eyes, this visage of eternal last moments. I see these walls around me now, the window with the view of the mountain, my sisters gathered at the bedside, studying the folds in the linen and trying not to look at my dying body. I have fallen down the well of these eyes and I swim in this body. St. Barbara hovers over me, the Blessed Virgin extends her hands. If it were only for a moment it would be a paradise before the true reward, but I am locked in these eyes, in this terrible mask. Paradise is a distant place.

I see him return, now and then. He doesn't stay long. Occasionally, our eyes will meet and there is something held between us. He has made preparations, bought supplies, cleared a wall of his apartment. Already he sees me there. There is only the painting left to be done.

Recollection

In my church the quiet seemed planned and had a meaning that helped me think and pray, but here the quiet is only itself, just silence. This church, Blessed Saviour, is Catholic and close to I-90, and it is that second reason, along with the fact that it was left standing, that got the FEMA people to choose it. Close to the interstate, easy to get to, the FEMA man said. Someone from town said that it ought to be held in an arena or a warehouse, even a vacant store—we got a lot of them—would have done. But the FEMA man reminded him and the group in general that the other spaces were being used for processing. That's a great word I've learned, *processing*. I've heard it before, of course, only never heard it used with people. Ned and I were processed by the national guardsman, who came looking to see if anyone was missing or hurt and then again by an insurance man for the damage to the roof. The dead folks were processed through a makeshift morgue in the junior high gym. Processed. It means forms and head counting I suppose, and a name as far as it isn't anybody else's name.

I didn't want this to be held here. I thought even a room at the Ramada, one of those little ballrooms would be nice, but there's no money for that. It is not that I don't like Catholics; it's not at all that, it is just that I am not partial to their churches. There is too much adornment; the stained glass and the silverware, all the candles; it's overwhelming. But it isn't a question of taste, it's more than that, it's really about what matters in a church, about looking inside you and I could never do that here, not with those grave faces of the saints looking down on me.

My church was destroyed in the tornado which touched down in Jefferson county forty miles to the east of here and then wound through Samson county, destroying Hatleyburg as it crossed the state line. Ned and I heard the alert on the radio and were in the basement when it passed through, shaking the house with a noise like a thresher, peeling shingles off the roof but leaving the frame and the rest of the house standing. We didn't even lose the lights, and I remember thinking it can't have been much of a storm to have the lights not go out. But five blocks away, less than a quarter mile, the post office and high school and most of the centre of town were destroyed. We were shocked, Ned and I, there in the calm afterwards that was soon broken by the sirens, looking at the buildings, fronts like caved-in faces, looking so bad that we didn't even notice that the church was gone. Destroyed is the wrong word; my church disappeared, like it was stolen or eaten and only the crumbs were left, scattered around the ground and mixed in with the whitewashed bricks and wooden splinters. I remember turning around, which seems to me to be a silly thing to do now, as if expecting to see my church, whole and intact, deposited on some other corner. I couldn't speak, Ned was shouting at me that we had to help, by this time there were fire trucks and ambulances roaring around us, but I couldn't move. I could not believe that it was gone. A person asked me if I was all right. She gave me a blanket. I suppose I must have looked a sight.

Later that night I watched it on the television, all the vans from the television networks with their little dishes on the top had arrived in town. I saw my neighbours interviewed and in the corner of the screen I saw our house, with its edge of roof missing shingles. I saw it all beamed up to some satellite and bounced back into my parlor. I would have gone to the window but then I couldn't have seen as much as I had on the television. Besides, I needed to stay in. Ned was out with a volunteer brigade but I couldn't find it in me to help right then, something stopped me. I sat at home and watched the television and looked at the lights. I turned them on and off and felt the dark like cold water against my face.

When Ned got home he was tired and quiet and for a long time we lay in bed without saying a word. I told him that I had called Kyle, our eldest who lives in Tulsa, to say we were fine. Ned didn't say a word and I hate to say it but I was glad for it, glad for the type of man he is that he can keep things he has seen to himself. I supposed that he had seen ruined things: homes and maybe even dead bodies and I couldn't bear to hear that, hear the names or the fact that maybe he had found a baby. That first night I didn't sleep at all until four in the morning and by the time I had woken up, Ned was gone. I tried to make breakfast but when I went to the sink all I could see was the mess that was now more evident in the morning light. Maybe I thought that it would all be better the next day, but I just stood at the sink looking out at the scraps of papers floating around outside. It was Sunday but I had nowhere to go.

The next day, when Ned came home for lunch, he suggested that I talk to somebody. He said that I had been quiet and that he was worried that I was suffering from stress. I just sat there and listened to him as he said this while he was eating his tuna fish sandwich. He was the one who wasn't talking, he was the one who was out at all hours with the volunteer crews while I was watching our home and taking care of him. You're the victim of stress, I said, and I accused him of not minding our home which made him stop eating, wipe his mouth, and get up to leave. I know that he was just trying to help but I didn't need to talk to anyone. I needed to have the things that sustained me to be brought back. I had my family. I was more fortunate than others, but I could not sleep at night for the thought that this had happened, that a path through town had been chosen and followed and people in its way had been killed and homes destroyed. I could not understand these things and in a way, and this seemed a shameful thing for me to say, I had moments when I was relieved that the church had gone because I felt I couldn't pray.

By that time the people had brought in a busload of psychologists and counsellors, so it was no wonder Ned had begun to talk to me about stress. But it wasn't for me, the talking. I wanted to clean my yard up. I wanted the dead and injured to return. I wanted my church back. The talking would do none of that, and so the next day I went out to start cleaning up. I started with our yard, back first, then the front and found for the first time that I felt comfortable being outside. I put everything into the garbage bag; litter, pages of homework, torn pages from newspapers, restaurant menus. The things I could not put in the garbage were the photographs. I was surprised by the first one I found, a snapshot of a woman standing next to a fountain. She was dressed in a beautiful summer dress, dark blue and judging from the style and the age of the picture it was taken in the sixties. I put the photo in the breast pocket of Ned's shirt that I was wearing. An hour later I found another picture, a school picture of a young boy, one of those two-by three-inch photographs that are cut out from a larger sheet, it had jagged edges where a safety scissors had been. I turned it over but it had nothing on the reverse side except for a stain of dried glue.

Over the course of the first day I found fourteen photographs; black and white photos of men in fedoras standing next to whale-sized cars, a portrait of a man in a military outfit (one of the few where identification was possible as his uniform had the nametag 'Schmidt' on it), a wedding picture of people I could not recognize, bride and groom holding the knife above the cake. I brushed away the dirt on one photo to find faces that I recognized: family at a picnic table; people from the Kiwanis; the Minters, from a house a couple of blocks away, a house no longer there. I went to the FEMA trailer and asked how I could find Ed Minter, who had lost his wife along with the house, and was told he was being lodged at the Rotary. As I walked over there I thought about whether it was a good idea or not to bring the picture to Ed. I didn't really know him that well or even have the chance to give my condolences on his loss and I thought that he might take it the wrong way, like I was bringing scraps of his life, his lost life, back to him. I found him at the entrance to the fire station, sitting on the front steps and staring at the streets now full of trailers and the parked cars of insurance adjusters. I shook his hand and told him that I was sorry and then gave him the photo, which was wet with the perspiration from my hands. He looked at it suspiciously at first; I suspected he had been having to read and sign a lot of official documents in the last few days. But his face softened, and not just because he was a good man but I'm sure because he knew me and what Ned and I had been through with Ned Jr. and for a moment I thought that I was the wrong person to bring this to him, that he might think I was bringing him into something private and unfortunate that only Ned and I shared and now had drawn him into. I was afraid because I had not felt pain for such a long time and didn't know how he would react to it. He brought his hand to his mouth as if keep something back and then closed his eyes and, covering them, cried. I sat down with him on the steps, hoping no one had seen me do this to him. I put my hand on his shoulder for a moment and just wanted go home when he reached out and touched my other hand and thanked me.

As I walked home I thought about the other photos and imagined them floating up in the tornado's wake, scattering around the county, faces looking out into nothing and nothing staring back. I always imagined loneliness as something peaceful but now I knew it could be something full of wicked energy and movement. I stopped and turned back towards the downtown and kept walking until I reached the door of the FEMA coordinator. He nodded when I told him what I wanted to do, that if he could spread the word around and have the photos forwarded to me, that I would try to return them. He took my name and address and thanked me.

By weeks' end I had hundreds of pictures. Bags of them arrived in FEMA and post office bags, people who had heard drove up with what they had found. We placed them on the dining room table until there was no room and then had to scramble to find places for the sacks. That was why we needed a place. That is how I came to the Blessed Saviour on I-90.

I am not that interested in pictures themselves. I take pictures and we have a scrapbook of Christmas photos and big events but I find we rarely look at it. I have always felt uncomfortable in photographs; I am the one squinting or with the pained expression supposed to be a smile. Those red pupils are usually mine. In the middle of all this, I had a chance to look back at our albums; Ned and me in Gainesville just after we got married; the twins, Kyle and Ned Jr., standing on a baseball bleacher the summer before we ever heard the word leukemia. Kyle's first day at school and then Jane appears, in a bonnet and then, magically on her three-wheeler, green-eyed and smiling for the camera like it is an old friend. But then, it was me behind the camera. There is something special about photographs, I have to admit; maybe it's the smell of age or the curling that happens to them when they're jammed up under the frame of a mirror. The textures change from washed out grays to grainy colour to the vivid shine and the border widens with the years until they disappear from photos in the mid-seventies.

I had hoped that by the time we had gotten permission to use the Blessed Saviour basement, Ned and I would have made up; and so, he would have become involved in sorting the photographs, which was really just looking at the photos, as I didn't have a complicated system to organize them. But he was silent, watching the sacks come into the house and grudgingly helping to load them into the van. I thought it best that we should just get a large space and spread the photos out on tables, removing those that had identifying marks (those we recorded in a registry book) and those that were unseemly. That being said we only managed to examine half of them, the rest would have to be sorted out by those who were looking for something or someone in particular. Ned spent his time working with the crews, exhausting himself with work.

He stopped talking, like he was grieving or more likely felt embarrassed for having not lost anyone to the tornado.

A Catholic church has unusual names. Father Michael showed me a room called the sacristy and we walked out to the centre of the church with its high vaulted ceiling. He showed me where they kept the communion wafers, which he called the blessed sacrament. He paused for a long time and I didn't know what I should do. I think he was praying, but I couldn't be sure; he was an older gentleman. He showed me the basement where the Catholic Women's League met and where they had parish meetings. We were in luck, he said, as there had been a family of four from Guatemala who had been staying in the parish basement until last week. He didn't say where they went. Along the side of the room were a number of long tables with folding legs that I knew would be perfect for the photos. I showed him a flyer with the times for viewing and identifying the photos, all under the title, Photograph Recollection, which was something suggested by a lady at FEMA. He looked at it for a long time and asked me why I had organized this.

I couldn't give him an answer, other than to say that it felt right and that I would have liked to have the opportunity to find something I'd lost. There were other reasons, the ones you can't say because they are hard to put into words: the eyes, always looking out at the invisible camera, the arms around each other, the heads crowded into the frame, the expectation. Some have people standing stock-still, with that smile I know, my smile. Others are blurred with movement, perhaps discarded but still beautiful.

We left the house at seven to drive to Blessed Saviour. Ned was still in bed until ten minutes before I had to leave, not stirring. He's a light sleeper and awakens before his alarm but now he lay motionless, telling me he needed the car and had other things to do but would drive me.

I met Father Michael at the steps of the parish centre. He unlocked the door and together we spread the unidentified photographs out on the table, at the end there were over a thousand of them, collected from six counties and two states, thrown into the air and scattered until they were brought here. We dumped photos onto the table and then spread them like dried flowers until the surfaces were covered. We turned over the upturned ones. Faces, faces. Staring back at me, silent. Moments captured and then set free, recollected now. Coming down the stairs there was someone with a video-camera, a news crew that wanted to talk to me about what was going on. There had been stories in the paper, along with advertisements, things that Ned had glanced at but turned the page.

I tried not to blink as they turned the lights on me. I imagined my eyes looking out, into the camera, into space. For a moment I felt like I was no longer there, then the television interviewer said thank you and the light turned off. We opened the doors and the crowds came in. Throughout the day crowds passed through, examining the photos and consulting each other. There were groups of women, young and old, families and couples as well as people who came alone. Some wept but didn't touch the photos, others gasped and shook their heads at what I felt must be the thought of all this personal material being wrenched from shoeboxes and keepsake chests and dispersed over the six counties. The last thing to do was to register the photos that had been recognized and record the name and phone number of the person who claimed them.

Two hundred and seventy five photographs were identified and recovered. Many people offered an explanation; they didn't have to but most did and I thought that they felt better for it afterwards. Twelve photos were of people who had died. Some of them I'd even recognized from other photos in the newspaper or on television.

Now the doors are closed. Father Michael has gone to dinner and given me the keys and I pause for a moment longer, unable to leave. The photos sit in layers like leaves fallen onto the ground. I walk down the rows between tables, rustling my hands through the pictures, my fingers brushing against faces and foreign sites, wondering if there is a photo of me, something someone has kept, in the years before I met Ned, something of me smiling into an unknown future. Among these pictures, all lost and staring up at the stars, is there a picture of Ned with someone he would have been more happy with, someone he could talk to, someone whose photo is all that remains and for whom he now secretly grieves? Everything is brought up into the sky and scattered; some are found and others are not, but most are looked for, cared for when they land on the ground. I think there must be a picture out there of my little Neddy, one I've never seen, his face among others at a birthday party. And then there are lives that I can never know, all those unclaimed moments, faces forever unrecognized, all of it silent here in the darkness, waiting to be lifted skyward again. I go upstairs to a church that is not my church. Its walls are covered in the light reflected from the stained glass. It's a quiet place for me to sit and wait for Ned.

The Blue Angel

The square of sunlight moves across the floor and climbs the bed where it grazes Remilliard's shoulder before fully enveloping his face, which gives a buggy twitch in the warmth. It's the hottest part of the day, if that can be said, as the icicles on the south side of the Hôtel St-Lambert begin to sweat in the noonday sun. It's the least cold moment, the least cold place, but this is momentary too. Remilliard awakens to the scintillations of sun and ice through the window and assumes a hangover is about to declare itself. He expects waves of nausea, tidal poundings of ache, but is surprised to find that nothing breaks; the other side of the room is dark and full of warm relief, like sleep itself, into which he turns.

The wake-up call rings in at 12:03 p.m. and he coughs a thank you as the operator flatly wishes him a happy New Year. He supposes that the hotel staff, surly with the holidays, think he is just another junkie sleeping the day away. He has made their renewed acquaintance for a week now, and they treat him with the standard professionalism one expects in a Quality Motor Inn. Although he is one of many transients he likes to imagine that to the staff his face somehow isn't that of the archetypal motor-inn guest—visages crusted with guilt and sleeplessness, an unspoken biochemical woe. But there is nothing to set him apart, and for that he knows he should be thankful. Every day Remilliard goes to the main reception desk to ask for towels or check for messages. But there is no recognition. And there are never messages for him (*just checking*, he will say, and this is truer than they know). Bringing the girl back with him last night should have changed their opinion of him, granting him the higher tier infamy of pimp, or dealer, bartering off a debt in the new economy of endorphins and sweat. But the eyes that meet his at the desk never seek explanation, they only glow with a sullen, service-industry fury that is directed inward. They don't see him as a villain. They don't see him at all.

She is there beside him, smaller and more-fragile looking than he remembers her being last night when they stumbled in. Remilliard tries to remember her name and thinks he heard her say it was Chantal—*for the hotel register I'll call you Mrs. Tremblay*, he said, to which he remembers her smiling. There must be a high season for them too, he thinks, tonight must be a big night, biggest of the year, like a convention everybody goes to.

He's in the shower when she wakes up. The door opens and she looks in and for a moment he's glad he brought his wallet into the washroom because he's heard about guys getting ripped off, clothes and all being stolen from the room. She tells him that she wants a cigarette, and when he tells her he doesn't have one her face sours. Remilliard asks her if she wants some breakfast or lunch and she agrees, sitting slumped on the toilet, holding her head.

Her name *is* Chantal, or so she confirms after a moment of conversational awkwardness as they take their place at a booth in the hotel's restaurant; and although she is the first prostitute he's slept with, he can imagine many of them would use Chantal as a name. But they're not called prostitutes now, he thinks, they want to be called sex-workers or sex-tradespeople. As Remilliard thinks about this what to call her what she calls herself, he's suddenly struck by the ease and beauty of his own breathing. *Phoo.* A slow, luxuriant expiration. He's then impressed by how stupid this thought is, and then how funny it is that he thinks that it's stupid, and finally that the feeling doesn't have anything to do with his breathing but must be something else entirely. By the time the coffee arrives Remilliard knows what it is. He's happy for the first time in months and it shows; he feels as though he is lighting up the room and everyone, including Chantal, basks in the energy. She might even consider it a compliment to her rehabilitative efforts of the night before.

He wants to ask her questions about her life: why someone would become a prostitute and what sort of life it is. But that seems phony and probably something she's heard from many customers who have suffered after-the-fact guilt and who pretended to be interested about her as a person and not because of what she promised in a more tangible, goods-and-services way. He doesn't know much about her except for the tattoo on her lower back and the calm way she walked him through the entire procedure, as though she were a tour guide to an exotic and potentially dangerous place, not wanting him to miss out on the sites but keeping him on the bus and in his seat. He can tell a few things about her, though. Chantal is young, he can see that, and hungry. She reminds him of a girl the morning after her prom who has stayed up for sunrise, looking out of place in her dress, the buzz of the big night not worn off. She spoons down scrambled eggs and is finished her cup of coffee and he hasn't even started into his yet. She catches him looking at her. She smiles.

"What are you smiling at?" Remilliard says.

"Good breakfast. Good coffee."

"It's more than that. Coffee doesn't make me smile like that."

"I really like coffee," she replies, more seriously than he expected.

The hotel restaurant is busy today, filling up with families and groups of older people. Remilliard has never been in a restaurant on New Year's Eve—at least not in the morning. He thought it would be empty. He and Chantal chat for a while. She tells him the vague details of her life: the plans to go back to school, the other job, that she wants to buy a motorcycle. He thinks of where she's from, probably a place an hour or two from Montreal, Saint-Jean-Chrysostome or some place like it, a place full of brothers and sisters whom she doesn't see anymore.

"A motorcycle?" Remilliard says, wanting the family to evaporate.

"Yeah. Maybe a Honda for a starter, but eventually I'd really want a Ducati."

"How do you know so much about bikes?"

"An old boyfriend. He used to fix them and raced a bit."

Around them a party of twelve—young adults, grandparents, strollers of weepy children—is ringmastered into place by a waitress and the harried parents. Remilliard looks at his watch, a nervous tic, a habit spasm from work.

"I recognized you," Chantal says to him, leaning back and putting out her cigarette in the ashtray.

"Excuse me?" he says.

"Why do you think I came up to you?"

Because I look pathetic, because I am lonely and would never have gone up to you. Because you could see that I am a man with enough money in my pocket and you are a business person willing to make a cold call.

He says nothing. A man in the party of twelve risks a sidelong glance at Chantal, who sits crossed-legged in her tight black dress, a wriggling leg dangling a clunky platform shoe. The man's wife then intercedes and directs a caustic glare at them, with most of the women at the table turning around in support. The air fills with a kind of static. Chantal is blissfully indifferent.

"I saw you in the paper," she says, smirking. "We were all talking about it. Seeing you there at the table with your friends, and when I danced for your buddy."

"Maurice."

"Yeah, whatever, I was looking at you because I thought it was you and once I got close I was sure."

The waitress comes over and their cups are refilled. Cold coffee rings the saucer under Remilliard's cup like a moat.

"And why did you come over to me?"

"I told you, I recognized you. You're famous."

"From where?"

"*Voyons donc*, from the paper. I read the paper, you know."

Someone has shut off the air in the restaurant, sealed the vents and closed the doors. Remilliard begins to take big breaths but can feel the oxygen disappearing.

"I get that a lot. That isn't me."

She leans in. "*I know it's you, mister.* I'm good with faces and names."

"No, it's a mistake."

"It's no mistake, hey, last night you fucked like you wanted to kill *me*."

"I haven't killed anyone," he says in a constrained voice. Remilliard fumbles for his wallet, leaning forward and brushing against the table, spilling more coffee into the saucer. He puts a twenty on the table.

"Come on, sit down," she says. "Bonne année."

Remilliard is up and out of the booth with a quick jack-knifing motion, pointing to the table for the waitress to let her know that he isn't dashing on the tab.

The man at the next table stares at his menu as though it were a ticking bomb he has been asked to defuse, devoutly refusing another glimpse at the companion Remilliard has just deserted. His wife maintains a surveillant scowl at Chantal, who nonchalantly takes her little finger, curls it around and under the strap of her minidress and runs it down from the collar-bone to the slope of her breast, lifting up the strap ever so slightly to expose a brown sector of nipple. She turns to the woman, puckers and winks.

Remilliard has gathered his belongings from the bedside table, signed his bill for the florid manager and has his car cresting the summit of the Champlain Bridge before he has the time to consider what he has done. He shouldn't have left: the hotel was an ideal place and he would have been able to stay another week. Ten days maybe. In front of him the city sits in plumes of exhaust and ice crystals, in the background he sees the outline of Mont Royal like the haunches of a vagrant, curled-up, seeking comfort and grill-space. A grey lucent haze builds around him, his breath armour-plating the windows in fog now that the defroster of his Hyundai has given up. *Tabernac.* All the car's vents shoot out cold air, a coy Korean automotive deity blowing kisses to him from behind the grills. He slams the dash a couple of times with his fist. Any heat that he felt through the window this morning or radiating from Chantal has been replaced by a marrow-soaking cold. He wants to get home.

He calls his St. Henri address his 'place' because the vagueness of the word somehow offsets the inherent squalor of a partially furnished three-and-a-half walkup apartment rented by a forty-two-year-old man. *Place.* His friends must laugh just as he does when they call their unheated winter cabins 'chalets'. He throws the door open and sweeps his hand along the near wall to catch the switch and a room appears: an incomplete set of patio furniture sitting on what he supposed must have been a hastily-laid parquet floor, missing slats as the pattern trails off to the corner; the gyprock pocked with scars of the previous tenants' domestic disputes, a kind of cave art. He was depressed by the place until he found that he could be alone here, away from work, away from a house emptied of his family. Home.

He puts his overnight bag on the kitchen table and sits down. He is this famous now, he thinks, recognized by prostitutes and chased from hotels. A celebrity, infamous for his bad luck; a weatherman who gets hit by lightning.

Since the start of his infamy he has kept the newspapers, arranging them into piles and keeping them in chronological order. The psychiatrist leaned forward when Remilliard admitted this months ago.

"Do you get enjoyment out of reading them?"

"No, I don't read them. I can't read them. They don't know me but they have all these theories about me. Pictures. I can't stand to see myself."

"But you keep them."

Remilliard nodded, shamed and exasperated, as though admitting to keeping a stash of porn.

"Where?"

"In a pile. In the closet."

"Why do you keep all these papers you don't read?"

"I suppose I need proof," Remilliard said, hoping his answer would get the psychiatrist to stop leaning forward. "Proof that this is happening to me."

The psychiatrist just stared, as though he expected a better explanation to come out of such a moment of high drama. Something more insightful. Diagnostic. Remilliard saw he was disappointed.

Now the newspapers sat in front of him on the table, where atop one pile a headline first pronounced his descent; how in January, almost a year before, the story of a twenty-four year-old man ending his life intersected with Remilliard continuing his, driving a Métro train down the green line to Honoré-Beaugrand. At Pie-IX Station the kid jumped. The jumper knew what he was doing, too, leaping off the near end of platform just as the train entered the station: maximum velocity, no chance to stop, barely seen with the light of the station bleaching Remilliard's retinas out of their tunneled darkness. They closed down the line in both directions, cops all over the place, psychologists too, all in full-dress corduroy, scouring around to console any stray witnesses. Remilliard was interviewed by a couple of cops. He remembered the big one had a leather sports jacket that made him look like a dealer. The older one wore a houndstooth cap, the type of hat he hadn't seen anyone wear in years. They both drank coffee and the big guy took notes. Remilliard told them that he didn't see much. Movement. Colour. He focused on the far end of the platform. He didn't mention to the cops that he could tell it was a young guy, that he thought he saw the flash of a face. He felt the impact and threw on the brakes, not pulling too hard because he knew that the kid must already be dead and he didn't want any passengers hurt. The cop flipped the notebook shut and looked at his partner. He gave Remilliard a look meant to convey that they had other things to do and they left.

After that, Remilliard called it a day. First, he stopped for a beer with Steve and Laurent before continuing home in time to have supper with Lise and the kids. That night in bed, when he mentioned in passing what happened earlier, Lise shot up and turned on the lights.

"Why didn't you say anything before?"

"Well, the kids..." Remilliard said, pleased and ashamed the lie that came so naturally from his mouth. He was amazed at how it had slipped his mind. "I didn't want to mention it in front of them." He thought of Amélie and Johanne sleeping in the next room, unaware of what had gone on that day and felt justified in his silence.

"Are you okay?" Lise said, looking alarmed, as though she were playing out the entire scenario in a little Métro station in her head. She winced.

"Yeah, fine," Remilliard said, "A little shaken up."

The psychiatrist made it clear he thought *this*—the initial lie, and the partial recognition of a peculiarity in his reaction—was a key moment. But in the next months Remilliard would find his entire life explained to him as a series of other such moments. Each constituted a point on a line that could then be solved like a geometry problem by the psychiatrist, a pleasant but watery-eyed anglophone who spoke French with an inexplicable Belgian accent so distracting that it persuaded Remilliard to switch to English. To Remilliard's surprise, his was a life succulent with meaning. All those twitches on the surface, every little lie or hesitation, all spoke to some sort of deeply repressed, volatile inner world. This proposition was at first denied by Remilliard: there was no inner world, no repressed rage, not that he knew of. The psychiatrist nodded appreciatively and wrote something down in his notebook, similar to the one that held the cop's thoughts.

The psychiatrist was not Remilliard's idea. But when the second jumper found the front of Remilliard's train, and then the third a week later, questions began to be asked. Remilliard's supervisor dropped by for a chat and gave him a card for the counsellor with the phone number underlined. The union steward came hard on his heels with his assertion that Remilliard didn't have to say anything if he didn't want to. But it was up to him, the steward said, and backed away as though Remilliard were about to take a swing at him. People were, after all, beginning to notice, the steward said. With all the scurryings around the platform after the third death—an elderly woman stepping peacefully onto the eastbound lane at the foot of his train as it passed through Peel Street Station—it was the cop in the leather jacket who had recognized Remilliard sitting on a bench on the platform and came up to him. *You again? Bad luck, eh mister?* To which Remilliard just stared back. *Hey, if it wasn't for the fact that these trains had to stay on their tracks we'd think you were behind this.*

"What did he mean by that?" Remilliard asked Steve later over a pitcher, after relating the cop's remarks.

"It's odd that it's always your train, that's all," Steve replied, looking around for Laurent, who had not returned to the table after going to the washroom, choosing instead to hang around the video lottery terminals at the back of the bar.

"I would say killing yourself is odder," Remilliard replied, emptying his glass and placing it on the table. Steve played with his watchband and nodded.

When a man with an unfilled prescription in his pocket became the next one to jump on the tracks in front of him, the oddness of it all became as clear to Remilliard as the likeness of himself that he saw through the little window of a newspaper box the next morning. A photo from work, and a tip, likely from the cop, who if he couldn't catch a killer or push some junkie around, would have his fun and some extra cash with a scoop like this. It was the fourth newspaper article of his collection, the one where he was tagged 'The Blue Angel', and it had more information about him than he'd ever thought could be collected. When he got home that night he found Lise at the door, wanting answers, and not just because the phone was ringing off the hook with queries and interview requests. Tears rimmed her lower lids. She pinched the bridge of her nose, trying to hold the tears back, but it was no use, and before Remilliard had his jacket off she was sobbing. She pulled away from him when he reached out.

"You told me nothing," she said, hiccuping little shrieks between the words.

They sat for a while on the bench in the front landing and he stroked her hand. He had no reply. She was right. He came home from work every day and put his experiences at work out of his mind. Wasn't that what he was supposed to do, though?—That was the question Remilliard posed to the psychiatrist, but all it got him was a discussion of the inadequacy of denial as a coping mechanism. The psychiatrist asked him again and again how he felt and when he sat stupefied for lack of a credible answer Remilliard realized he was going into the file as denying or wilful or whatever psychiatrists call silent people whose silence is not desired. More sessions were scheduled, and then Lise was asked to come along as though to coerce a confession from him. Three times a week, sessions were held in the little office, with Remilliard dully seething, as now every action taken and word spoken in their marriage was brought out and examined like a body unexpectedly found floating in the lake. *What did it mean?* he was asked, now by both of them. If Remilliard was guilty of withholding from the psychiatrist then Lise more than took up the confessional slack, and in his office that overlooked the Nôtre-Dame-des-Neiges cemetery she found her voice as an archivist of her every disappointment. Such a memory. The psychiatrist was impressed, so would have Remilliard been had not the details been so personal and unremitting. Why had they gone to Thetford Mines for their honeymoon? Why had he, with a drawer full of coloured socks, every morning before work chosen the white pair? Why did he not react with grief when people started flinging themselves under the wheels of his Métro train? They both wanted to know. Lise and the psychiatrist bonded immediately, of course. This irritated Remilliard more than just because it would be two-on-one. He knew the strongest alliances were formed when there were grievances or obsessions to be shared. They seconded each other's opinion and shared glances of acknowledgement. She accepted kleenex from him and complimented him on his continental accent. And although neither would say it in front of him, to Remilliard they both seemed to come to the agreement that her husband had secrets, and this hidden life, and its concealment, could only mean more betrayal, a larger and more terrible world of undiscovered perfidy.

Through it all, he kept driving. From the east end to LaSalle he ran the train back and forth along the green line without delay or incident, ignoring the administration's request for him to take a leave of absence and turning away from the tabloids that now considered his indifference to be as charismatic and ominous as that of any biker kingpin whose exploits usually graced the front page. But on an afternoon shift in April, five weeks since anyone had committed suicide in front of him and at the moment when he allowed himself to think he could put it behind him, it happened. Pulling into the S-curve of Lionel-Groulx Station he initially saw nothing atypical—a line of people arrayed along the edge of the platform as though about to drink from a trough, some looking straight ahead, others staring at fellow passengers. But out of this crowd a pair of eyes emerged, flaring out their vaguest intentions. A young man forced eye contact. Then the hand came up with a thumb extended. He appeared to be alone on the edge until a young woman beside him lifted her arm into an identical salute and then took the free hand of her partner. The boy mouthed the words *Blue Angel* and smiled. A face of pure, inspired happiness. And then the two of them slammed into the windshield of Remilliard's driver's compartment.

For the moment that he was outside, in the time it took to hustle him from the entrance of the station to the waiting Société de Transport car, Remilliard was dazed by the strobing of flash-bulbs and heat of the television crews' lights. There would be no press conference, the spokesman for the Administration said, and ducked into the second car that squealed off into the night. At the downtown office with a view of Montréal, Remilliard was introduced to the superintendent, a smooth functionnaire with authoritatively tonsured hair the colour of gun-metal. He was directed to the chair across the table from the superintendent.

"According to your dossier, you've had several accidents recently, Mr. Remilliard."

"I have never had an accident."

"Six people are dead."

"These were suicides," Remilliard replied. He tried not to writhe in his work clothes. He wanted a shower, the security of water flowing from somewhere to somewhere: "I would like to have a union representative here before I say anything else."

"Monsieur Meursault is here," the superintendent said, jutting a dimpled chin at someone over Remilliard's shoulder. "René, do you have anything to say to Mr. Remilliard?" Silence. Remilliard swivelled to confront the face but the room's intense halogen lights blinded him. He turned back to the superintendent. "Well, then, we'll begin by saying that several people are dead and all the deaths have occurred on your train."

"I would like to speak to a lawyer," Remilliard said, gently running his fingers over the skin of his forehead, abraded by the pellets of tempered glass that had rained down on him after the impact. He tried to remember how many people he saw when he came into the room but understood whatever the number, he was alone here.

"This isn't a legal hearing, Mr. Remilliard. This is a debriefing."

And with that Remilliard was told of his reassignment, away from trains, electrified guide bars and volatile, impressionable youths. He was told that the papers, which usually did not report suicides, had found the coincidence of his being the driver for all the deaths so compelling that they rescinded their usual editorial policy. This was a problem, the superintendent said, as Remilliard was now some type of 'personality' for these unfortunate citizens, for these unstable young people, of whom many more, no doubt, existed. He was therefore a liability to the Société de Transport. His union, which in the past had gladly taken any opportunity to harass the Société, was now however in the midst of a particularly rancorous collective agreement renegotiation and viewed Remilliard as an embarrassment as well. And so, Monsieur Meursault remained silent in the shadowed back of the room, enjoying the new non-aggression pact negotiated over Remilliard. It was agreed that neither the Société nor the union needed more bad publicity, especially about the notorious lethality of one of their drivers. But Remilliard should not worry, the superintendent said, he would be looked after.

He was boarded at the Hôtel St-Lambert for the first of many respites, while the press and public scrutiny calmed down. He had time to think and now that Lise was no longer answering the phone, he had even more time. Several times during that week-long internment in the hotel he wished that he could talk to Tintin the psychiatrist and hear his Belgian accent, not for any therapeutic reason, but just for the conversation. An official from the Société de Transport called twice a day, always at the same hour, to ensure he was in his room. He would answer on the sixth ring and for a moment allow himself the conceit that this was an act of defiance. When the week was up he returned home to find Lise and the children gone, a note saying that she had to think about things, something better accomplished at her sister's house in Sorel. He wandered through the house, reading and re-reading the note. She wrote in a scrawl almost unrecognizable to him for the tremor that emotion must have placed in her hand, but even with the unsteady lines the message was clear: she could not be with a man so incapable of expressing his feelings, of hiding the truth. She continued, saying that he had changed and that this change was too much for her to bear. That night, lying in their bed, he opened all the windows in the hope that a breeze would blow through and that a sound would be created that he would mistake for the sound of his children playing or his wife in the next room. But the night was still and the house was enormously quiet around him. Before he fell asleep, he thought of the people who had jumped in front of his train and for a moment felt anger towards them: the young man and the lonely immigrant, the old woman and the depressed man, the couple. He saw their faces, eyes glossy as they made their pilgrimage to the platform's edge, and he cursed all of them that they had somehow conspired to take what he valued away from him. Then he cursed himself for thinking such things.

He still saw the faces a month later as he steamed like a *moule* in his little ticket kiosk at Station Vendôme, arguing with pensioners about ticket prices and exchanging glares with the loitering Haitian kids in the loose jeans who circulated through the station. It isn't so bad, the union steward said, mentioning to Remilliard the reallocation bonus that had appeared on his paycheque to sweeten the deal. He hadn't noticed.

Remilliard had tried his best to patch things up with Lise, working the phone like a stranded salesman, trying to regain the confidence of her sister in hope that the messages would be passed on. He continued going to the psychiatrist in hope that she would appear again. She didn't. The psychiatrist, perhaps lamenting the loss of a therapeutic ally, reoriented his focus, and Remilliard found himself having to discuss his newly-failed marriage at length. It could be a sign of his underlying unresolved problem, the psychiatrist said. Remilliard nodded. It was easy to nod. *Yeah, it could be.*

By September, Remilliard had moved in with his father after deciding that Lise and the kids would be better off in the house. He felt guilty at first approaching his father with his request, even if it was temporary, as since the death of his mother, he rarely saw the old man any more. However, his father had always been gracious about their lack of contact, his son had a job and a family, his life had intervened. But while he made the offer of his spare room willingly, it didn't take long before they had both begun to commit the little violations of enforced cohabitation. After the first two weeks, once the talk of hockey and weather was over and all the other buffers of personality exhausted, they faced the inventory of new smells and noises, the logistics of shared space. Remilliard was shocked at how run-down the place had become since his mother's death, how the curtains never opened and the sink was continually full of dishes, stacked and stinking. His father had changed too, lost weight and acquired that tired rheumy look that settles on men when they outlive their wives. His father had always had a certain pride, or at least that was the way Remilliard had seen it, but now the old man seemed satisfied in the lesser orbit of his home, peering into the television, occasionally sitting on the back patio and rocking gently on one of the kitchen chairs.

His father never asked him about the suicides or Lise leaving him, though. It was a relief to sit with someone and not have them ask questions; even Laurent and Steve had begun to treat him like a minor freak-celebrity so that now he didn't even have the sanctuary of the brasserie at the end of the day. He would pick up a six-pack at the dépanneur and together he and his father would sit in silence as the old man went through the channels with a regular, soothing benediction of the remote.

They were watching the weather forecast, a satellite shot of clouds arranging into a circle, about to whip-crack a hurricane down the Carolina coast, when Remilliard thanked him for being so understanding. The old man looked at his son for a moment, the remote motionless in his hand, and then got up and left the room. Remilliard sat alone, as though he had spoken to a ghost. The clouds on the television spiraled into a tight coil and appeared ready to drag the ocean toward the shore.

The summer extended itself, seeping into September like a warm stain through which Remilliard waded, making the short voyage between his ticket booth and spare room of his father's apartment. He was settling into a rhythm, he told himself. He thought about establishing some sort of exercise regime, joining a gym or buying a new pair of those jogging shoes. But instead he took to sitting in his room, installing himself there after taking his dinner in front of the television with the old man. His father would knock on the door and ask him how he was, worried that the drugs that permeated the neighbourhood had found their way into his house, and Remilliard would say that he was all right or that he was just tired.

He looked out the window that opened up onto the back lane. From his room he could see into other houses, where people would appear for a moment in their window frames and then disappear. The only distraction on his wall was a calendar from a few years back and Remilliard lifted the pages to look at all the dates, all the days gridded and organized into rows, all of it now gone. In eight months he had lost everything, and been unable to prevent all those losses as though his life had been a skid on an icy road, just something full of inevitabilities and frightful velocity. His wife once loved him, she had to have loved him once because all that they had could not have been built on misunderstandings. But there were eight months of days that told him otherwise. His father rapped on the door, a solid double-knock, reserved enough so that Remilliard knew the old man still had confidence in him, but wanting to know that he was all right just the same.

Once the view from his window and the calendar had lost their appeal, he turned his attention to the boxes that were lined up along the edge of the wall. He found old newspapers and mementos, photo albums with pictures of him and his brothers at their hockey tournaments, a picture of all of them next to the station wagon somewhere outside of Weyburn, Sasketchewan. He remembered the trip out to the Pacific Ocean that summer: cigarette smoke and an oceanic nausea, the heat rising from the black macadam as it split the prairie into two perfect, golden halves. Among the yellowed newsprint and curved polaroids he pulled out a souvenir book from Expo 67. He sat on a box and placed the book on his lap. On the cover, a woman dressed in an Expo 67 uniform, a blue stewardess-like outfit and an oblong hat, posed demurely in front of the huge geodesic dome built for the American pavilion. A monorail track cut an elegant French curve through the background. Inside there were the familiar pictures, the excitement of opening day, the flags from all over the world and all the visitors. His mother took all of them down to the exhibition site on Île-Sainte-Hélène every day of their summer vacation. All Remilliard could remember was the expression of wonder on every face, that they were standing on an island that had risen out of the river to become the centre of the world. But while his family looked around in amazement at the world spread out and on display, Remilliard marveled at the ground under them, knowing exactly where the earth for the man-made island came from, how it was hauled from the newly dug tunnels for the Métro lines. For Remilliard, the miracle of that summer began with the opening of the first Métro station on October 18th, 1966, his eighth birthday, which he firmly believed was no coincidence but most certainly something ordained, and for him the thrill of that Expo 67 summer reached its peak every morning as his family passed through the turnstiles and boarded the great blue Métro trains. In the months before the start of Expo, the rest of the line opened at the rate of a new station every six weeks, extending from under the St. Lawrence River to the furthest edges of downtown, glancing off Westmount before it headed toward LaSalle. As a boy, Remilliard could not sleep at night, thinking about the trains, imagining that he could hear them roaring through their tunnels. He loved the feeling of the train coming into the station, the emergence from the tunnel and the wake of the wind that blew his hair back as he stood holding his mother's hand on the platform. But it was the trains themselves that captivated Remilliard, they were a vision of the future: sleek and sparkling, powder blue, with rubber wheels like the Paris Métro and not the squealing, metal-wheeled railroad cars that tortured commuters in New York or Toronto. He recalled the thrill of the automatic doors opening to allow his family inside where they sat on the molded seats, none of them able to keep still with the excitement as they picked up velocity into that first tunnel.

Remilliard turned the pages. There was a special section on the Métro system, with photos of each new station, whose design had been commissioned to a different Québec architect, every one with its own unique features that spoke to its neighbourhood or a moment in history. Folded in the centre of the book was a map of the planned system. It was a grand vision, lines extending out like tentacles off the island and into the suburbs, four stations alone in Laval, a line reaching the airport. Ten lines in all, of which only four had eventually been built. The money, which was the real word for the will, had disappeared into the sink-hole of the Olympics and Montréal had seen its last station open in 1988. Now, to talk about extending the Métro to Laval was to be met with a circumspection reserved for religious people who roamed airports. Still, it was a beautiful thing, and when he told his father that summer of his wish to be a driver on the Métro, the old man smiled because no one capable of feeling could deny the attraction of that compartment at the head of blue train.

It was decided for him that summer, and so it came as no surprise to his family when, ten years later, he announced his plans, unchanged, at his high school graduation. He applied for a position with the Société de Transport and within six months he was piloting his own train, first on line number five and then, after a couple of years he moved onto the great U-shaped circuit of line number two. For the last decade though, he had been a driver on the green line, line number one, the great line that ran from the dark heart of English WestEnd suburbs, through the downtown, past the Olympic tower that he cursed for stunting the Métro, and into the east end. It was the great line, carrying the bulk of commuters to McGill or on to Berri-UQAM, where three lines intersected and people disembarked to fan out all over the city.

On their first date, he and Lise took the Métro. He wasn't embarrassed and he thought that if she were, then it would be as telling as any other habit or opinion that would appear later. He remembered that date, the ride downtown to a movie, the pride that he had in where he worked, in what he did. He hoped that she would understand that about him.

Things were different now. Homeless people vied with busking musicians for the warmest spots in the Métro when the winter settled in and the stations themselves wore signs of neglect: the analog clocks on every platform had been dismantled or sat out of order and every corner was defaced by graffiti tags. But he loved it, the pull of the acceleration, the smooth ride, the feeling of passengers entering and leaving in a continual ebb and flow that made him think that he was part of a larger, living thing. Above him the city had gone through its usual tumults, the festivals and Stanley Cup riots, a couple of referenda for a country coming apart and staying together. He lived his life moving under it all, snaking through the tunnels, filling and emptying of zealots and fans and people, sensing the energy of each body passing through his great blue train. All those lives, all those intersections. He had once seen a film in high school about the human heart and he remembered all those little red blood cells traveling through capillaries, all lining up single file. Going somewhere, coming back. How could he tell that to the psychiatrist?

The next day, after buying La Presse and scouring the classifieds for an apartment, he called the union shop steward to notify him that he was filing a grievance. In a union with thousands of employees, conflicting schedules, and ergonomically blasphemous chairs, grievances were common and there was a process to be followed, Remilliard was told. What was not part of the process was the call from Monsieur Meursault, the union boss himself, later that afternoon, to clarify specific points of the grievance. Was it a matter of the reallocation bonus? No, that was fine, unnecessary even, Remilliard said. He just wanted to drive, he wanted out of that goddamn hamster cage in Vendôme Station and if he couldn't drive he would have to do something else; at that point Remilliard's voice trailed off, letting Meursault imagine him going to the papers and stirring up the pot again. Remilliard knew that their union had settled their contract favourably and that Meursault, like any victorious union boss, was capable of a conqueror's largesse that would make him view more charitably the request of a faithful employee. Meursault was silent for a long time, and Remilliard held on, saying nothing, letting the silence build like a sneer and thrilled to be able to hear the semi-laboured breathing of his union boss at the other end. Meursault said he would see what could be done, was that enough? For now, Remilliard said, and hung up the phone.

Within a week Remilliard had found a place in St. Henri and the first phone call he received after connecting the phone in his new apartment came from the union shop steward telling him that the grievance was settled and that he would be resuming work. He wanted to tell his father or phone Lise on the off-chance that she would accept his call, but instead decided to clean the shower and fix up the bathroom cabinet whose doors yawed open on their hinges as though in perpetual surprise that someone could live there. Remilliard was ecstatic after the first week of his return to the green line but when he sat down for a beer with Laurent and Steve he felt for the first time an unease that couldn't be dispelled even by the time they had finished their third pitcher of Boréale Rousse. He felt like celebrating but his friends were acting like he was some sort of outsider, coming in and spoiling their good time.

It was as if they begrudged him his good mood or the one reversal of the shitty luck that had collared him in the past year. If they didn't like their jobs, that was their problem, Remilliard thought; he needed his, and not for money or an extra pitcher of beer at the end of a day. They all sat quietly, watching a big screen television that showed highlights of the Canadiens' training camp scrimmages. He needed his job. He didn't have anything else. On the screen the action was interrupted when a fight broke out between two players, a journeyman and some hulking kid trying to break in with the club. The pair circled, then grabbed jerseys and exchanged blows until one went down, the other following on top, right arm pumping like a piston.

"They don't have much of a team this year," Laurent said, draining his glass.

Remilliard staggered home, happy not to have to negotiate his Hyundai through the streets with such a dysphoric buzz. He stopped at an intersection near the street where his father lived and looked down the back lane behind the old man's place. He caught a glimpse of his father in the lane, facing away from him, standing still. For a moment he thought the old man was urinating against the fence, that this was the first sign of some senility that would lead to an old-folks home or hospital hallway. He was about to call out to him when the old man turned sideways, bent down and patted a small black dog that he had at the end of a leash. He smiled and pulled a plastic bag out of his pocket as the dog got up from its crouch. They walked away. Remilliard continued home. Remilliard's good fortune lasted two and a half weeks, or four hundred hours, as *Le Journal* and *Hebdo Police* calculated for full dramatic effect. Four hundred hours was all that it took the Blue Angel to strike again, this time a commuter dead of a heart attack while he dozed on Remilliard's train. The paper went on—to Remilliard's disbelief and despair—that now the *Blue Angel* did not even need the victim's consenting death-leap but only had to make the offer of a ride on the death train to an unwitting commuter. In the next day's paper, details of the victim flowed like blood from a wound: a good worker, a family man, a taxpayer—a portly man no doubt swimming in cardiac risk factors, thought Remilliard, conveniently forgotten in the beatific stampede. *An Innocent Victim!* the headline read, below which Remilliard's red-eyed ID photo was twinned with the victim's wedding day picture as though he had martyred the man for the thrill of it.

Meursault was fairly explicit in his letter to Remilliard. There were two options, a half-pension and the promise of placement with another public service union or to accept a desk job with the Société de Transport. *Point final.* A response was required in twenty-four hours or it would be assumed that he had chosen the first option. He chose the second and was assigned to a metal desk in a windowless bunker filled with a collection of fellow burnouts, fuck-ups, and underachievers, where forms were processed and re-processed according to some unknowable protocol and where he first felt the need to suppress the urge to bring a gun to work. This was his life now, he thought, and adjusted his office chair carefully. It hadn't helped; after three months his whole body ached for having to sit at the desk. He lost weight without necessarily meaning to and would wake up hours before dawn, wondering where he was and then, resignedly, remembering.

Remilliard closes the paper. It is the last one in his collection, in which an editorial endorses his reassignment to a position where no further accidents can occur. Public safety is as much about perception as reality, it goes on to say, and although Mr. Remilliard has not been convicted of any crime he has lost the confidence of his co-workers, the union, the Société de Transport and the public. Meursault and the superintendent are commended for their willingness to listen to public opinion on the matter. There is a photo with the two of them, old adversaries now united on the Remilliard question, standing in the Guy-Concordia Station. The background of the photo is blurred by commuters moving too quickly to be registered by the camera.

It is the last night of the year and Remilliard cannot wait for it to be over. He should consider some resolutions but thinks better of it; if he has taken to drinking a little too much, well, who cares whether a form is filled out properly? There will be other forms. He hasn't seen his children in months; the last time they responded to him as though he were in some way probationary, as though his name had appeared on some register. He was astounded and saddened. Chantal was right. He hadn't realized it then, but he had become a man who could not be trusted. Even last night, when he was invited out by his former driver colleagues for their year-end supper and to a club after, he felt that he was not a regular guy anymore, not Luc Remilliard. Half of them around the table had gone to the press to sell their own little vignettes of the Blue Angel, and now they had the gall to sit there and act like he was some sort of misfit. Now he was different. He was dangerous. Chantal saw that: at the club later, as Maurice drank himself stuporous and tried to stuff two-dollar coins into her lamé panties, she recognized Remilliard and decided right then and there that she wanted to take a ride on the death train. Perhaps the psychiatrist was right, keeping the newspapers around to make him feel important was sick, but it was sicker if they didn't make him feel important. If he didn't think his reputation was earned, well then, too bad. It was his. It was him.

He sorts through the mail and turns on the television. For the past few days he has re-entered the public domain through a series of year-end news recap shows. His story has it all: from the sad facts of the suicides and the tragedy of the last victim to the undeniable fascination with the coincidence of his role in the deaths, and finally, the added 'where are they now' feature of his reassignment. It was this renewed interest that led the Société de Transport to farm him out to the south shore hideaway in hopes that he would wait out the festivities in complete, hotel-room anonymity. They called it his Christmas bonus.

He presses the flashing light on his answering machine and

hears Maurice's voice, woeful and pleading for him to call. He has a certain fondness for Maurice, not just because Maurice has the unusual feature of conveying whatever emotion he is feeling through his facial expressions without modification and so in spite of his impressive stupidity, he can at least be trusted not to be able to lie. He was the only one to talk with Remilliard last night, even Steve and Laurent busied themselves in conversations with others. *Ah Maurice*, Remilliard thinks, such a look of wonder as you sat there and asked about the deaths, what sadness unfolded on that mug as you were told of the divorce. Later on, Maurice wore a frozen grin of dumb-lust as dancers came over to their tables. He asked Chantal to marry him and Remilliard was certain, if only from Maurice's facial expression, he would have gone through with it had she accepted.

He dials the number and Maurice answers, croaking in pain. He woke up in a snowbank, almost froze to death and, *tabernac*, he's sick. Maurice wants to know if Remilliard will take his shift tonight.

"I can't, Maurice. You know that."

"But they'll fire me if I call in sick tonight, even the union has warned me."

"Don't you have any sick days left?"

"They were all gone in September, do you remember I had the kidney stone?" Maurice coughs, something rattling—full and high-pitched at the same time, like a car alarm thrown into a pot of soup. "My sick days are gone for the year, fuck if it wasn't a leap year too or I would be home free. You've got to help me out."

"I can't," Remilliard says softly.

"They'll fire me," he pauses and Remilliard hopes he won't cough again. "One night, not even that, one shift."

"I'll need your ID."

"It's here waiting for you."

Maurice opens the door and Remilliard instinctively steps back, the guy looks so bad. His voice was lousy but it doesn't do him justice. He stands with a blanket up and around his head. The open door billows out steam around him.

"You should go to a hospital, man." Remilliard says, worried that Maurice won't take him seriously.

"I was there this afternoon, I got my first dose of antibiotics on a stretcher in the emergency room."

"They didn't keep you there?"

"No beds. I can walk, so I was asked to walk."

They stand in the billowing steam, Maurice extends a blanketed arm and passes him his ID.

"Bonne année, Luc."

On the way to Angrignon Station, the westernmost end of the green line, Remilliard begins to worry about the repercussions should he be caught. Having moved through Métro stations and work checkpoints so casually all his life, he is now forced to consider the sequence of his actions as though it were all part of some caper: parking the car, opening the drivers' entrance-door, passing the ID though the detector, and for a moment it all seems immensely complicated, as though he were suddenly aware of what something previously thought automatic actually entailed. But he will not be caught, he reasons, because he looks the part and has a valid ID and besides, if it was a crime it was one that nobody would have thought was important enough to bother committing.

But he takes no chances, walking into the station with eyes averted and head down so that no one will recognize him; but after a few steps it is apparent that this is uncalled for as the station is nearly empty and those working are completely absorbed in that self-protective glazed-eye look he has seen before on hotel clerks and psychiatrists. He passes through the ID checkpoint without incident and walks to the platform where his train awaits. Here, the trains transfer laterally to the opposite line and begin their return trip. His pulse picks up, as though it were something attached to the line, feeling the amperage bringing him back to life.

Around him the tempered glass of the compartment curves and the outside world elongates in a familiar way. There has always been glass in the way, he thinks, something giving him the impression that he was seeing things as they were but in fact refracting the world on him. Keeping him from it. There was a time when Remilliard ruminated on the loss of his family and job, when he fantasized about such a night as this, wanting it to be full of a terrible, confirming mayhem, daring every freak and the black-eyed goth kid to experience what they had wrought on him, something that would leave everyone satisfied. But that dream has left him, evaporating like his breath tonight.

Now he thinks about traveling through the places he loves, looking at the faces of people passed and indicating to them, with a nod or maybe just with eye contact, that he knows something about their lives, the contingencies and moments without explanation. He wants to tell them that they are watching him through glass, but he is there. He is driving their train.

The door closes and he knows that he cannot in any meaningful way be stopped now. He is in the driver's compartment, controls for the doors and the rheostatic mechanism that pulls the train forward all within his reach. The gleaming blue train advances toward the platform where it will pick up the first of the shift's passengers. On a night like tonight there are a few solitary riders already waiting. Sentinels here, welcoming him.

American Standard

Nathan is on a roll. "Do you know what determines the rotational direction of movement?"

Wayne gives Nathan not so much as a side-view glance as he guides the truck along the outer lane of Highway 401 to Windsor. But Nathan is working Wayne's peripheral vision; he positions his hands, motioning with one above the other as if to unscrew a pickle jar. He is trying to describe something and cannot—will not—be ignored, hard as Wayne tries. "It's called the Coriolis effect, you know," he says, returning his hands to his lap. "It's the same reason hurricanes blow clockwise and tropical storms in the southern hemisphere go the other way. Same story with toilets when you flush."

With that, Nathan becomes silent for the first time in the hour since they left Sarnia. For Wayne, the haul itself from Sarnia to Windsor and then on to Ann Arbor is a short hop, not worth a second thought; and the risk involved in getting past customs, well, he had slept poorly all week because of that, but Nathan was the cross to bear that he hadn't foreseen and he groans under the burden of having to restrain himself from throwing the pain-in-the-ass out of the moving truck.

"Where'd you learn that?" Wayne says, parlaying the misery of chitchat. "Community college?"

"No. I watch the Weather Channel." There is a hint of offence Nathan's reply.

Oh Christ, Wayne thinks, if he's sensitive he should have just kept the hell quiet. Of course Shirley would disagree, but then

Nathan was her cousin and she had probably become immune to such chatter through years of holiday family dinners with roomfuls of Nathans, nattering factoids from behind cobs of corn while they awaited plates of sliced turkey. She would say that he was just a kid and that Wayne should cut him some slack, and then she would smile for a moment, making all the Nathans of the world mute. But she had her hard side too, glaring at Wayne when he stumbled in late on a Saturday, or when he failed to return with one of the new jobs after the petrochemical plant expanded. That look she had, he couldn't describe it. It was an expression as familiar to Wayne as her soothings, as personal. More.

Shirley would say that he was lucky to have Nathan riding with him, to which he would have no response, because if she thought Nathan was a boon, she was beyond understanding how deeply he had been affected by Mike's departure. Mike—who occupied the passenger seat for the last two years, speechless and huge as a flannelled Buddha—had been his friend and then boss and finally, partner, until departing for a job at the Windsor Casino; thus leaving the door open for the Nathans of the world to enter and commence their water torture. Nathan had not been sitting beside him for five minutes when the questions started: Why were they taking the 40, anyway, when they could have crossed over to Michigan right away at Sarnia? When Wayne countered that it really made no difference to him, mentioning his experience and, if Nathan had forgotten, his position as the owner-operator of the rig, Nathan seemed unimpressed. The younger man pressed the point, further advocating the American route, saying that, actually, there was a considerable difference, a savings of a hundred kilometres if they had crossed over at Port Huron, and then there was the savings on gas and the roads, those seamless concrete interstates, well, the truck would almost drive itself. All Wayne could say was that they had an awful lot of toll highways down that way, and the extra wait at the booths and toll costs could set them back. They were past Chatham now, anyway, and they would be in the

States soon enough. And, Wayne said, in a tone of summation he felt entitled to not just as owner-operator but as Nathan's employer, *he* wanted to pass through Windsor.

A mist falls, speckling the windshield, but Wayne can't decide whether or not to turn on the wipers. Same with the radio, he wants to turn it on and play something loud but at the same time the thought of music and DJ patter seems worse than Nathan. Nathan starts talking about the u.s., about Michigan specifically, discoursing about public policy on zebra mussels and recent EPA rulings until Wayne begins to suspect that he must be an idiot savant—and not a piano playing drooling fool or one of the quiet ones whose eyes rolled back like tumblers as they recited the day of the week of any given date in the last thousand years—but a more pernicious one, personalized, proximate.

"….and that's the reason for it, really. It all comes down to a water conservation clause."

"What?" Wayne says, fiddling with the radio dials.

"When the EPA initiated the water conservation clause it essentially banned the use of the fourteen litre toilet in the United States."

"All I know is that we've got a delivery to make. Gotta go to the u.s.a."

Like any Canadian living close to the border, Wayne admitted a certain flexibility in his opinions of Americans and their country, reversals often occurring depending on the topic or his mood. In the same sentence he could decry American arrogance or marvel at their brash sense of destiny, he had interpreted their openness as refreshing naiveté and as thundering global idiocy, depending on the context. America: it offered so much that it was easy to feel one way or another about it, but that didn't make it any less confusing. America was perfect freedom and lethal injections; a distant bounty, endless strip malls offering hollow-point ammo and Kevlar vests: it was a promise that a person could change and a warning of what that change could be. And as Wayne steered his truck toward the border he felt that at that moment he disliked Americans more than he disliked Nathan. At times like this the universe of America—whose citizens he had sporadically encountered, whose values he watched rain down from a heaven of satellites—coalesced for Wayne into a single theoretical family of four: mom, dad, son, and daughter, between them personifying the great republic's every nasty twitch and tic. When he thought of America, he imagined *them*, and hated their loud semi-bellowing and the fat children who bellowed in a higher register. He was galled by the way they flashed their money and always complained about what they got in return or the way they seemed to crush everything underfoot. He didn't tell Shirley but the reason he refused to take a job at the Windsor Casino was that he didn't want anything to do with Americans on a regular basis, even if it was helping to steal money from them. He was offended by their voracity, their belching, befouling appetites, even if those appetites fed the desire for the truckload of fourteen-litre standards that he was hauling. They stole our hockey teams and drinking water and now they were stealing our toilets, he thought, and if there wasn't an envelope of cash at the close of the deal and Shirley waiting at home with her contingencies, he would have let the Americans shit into a sink.

Nathan didn't have to give Wayne the state-of-the-union spiel about over-sized toilets either. Wayne's brother Gordie had taken over the plumbing business when their dad died ten years before, and for the past five years Americans had been coming into the shop to buy big flush units. Before they had their big fight, when Wayne worked the service and supplies counter in the shop, he had seen a couple from Saginaw wander in, pretending to browse but so fidgety that you'd think they were hunting up a monster rock of crack cocaine. He had listened as they explained their predicament. He hooked them up with what they needed. The pilgrimage began in earnest after the American Energy Policy Conservation Act of 1992 came into effect, banning the sale of toilets with a flush capacity of anything more than six litres, and plumbing shops all along the border were only too happy to help their southern neighbours in their yearnings to be free of whatever wretched refuse plagued them. In the quiet economy of hygiene, the big flush models were the blue-chip performers, and Wayne's back had ached in anticipation with each approaching weekend at the thought of loading the jumbo toilets into the trunks of day travelers from the states.

Naturally, he wanted Nathan to know as little about what they were hauling as possible. He could see Shirley now, incensed and embarrassed at having to call a lawyer to bail them out and, while she had him on the line, maybe just sounding him out about how assets were split in a divorce. He thought the whole deal had been blown when they were loading and one of the bowls toppled and hit the ground, splitting open like a huge human skull. The kid figured it out pretty quick, looking at the bowl and the installation instructions, which clearly gave its specs highlighting the luxurious fourteen liter flush, and then looking at the phony six litre box the bowl had been repackaged in. Wayne told him he could get out then, swore him to secrecy. To his credit Nathan didn't hesitate. He just shrugged and hoisted the next box into the truck. Now, Nathan was holding forth about the EPA and U.S. environmental policy—which didn't surprise Wayne as he guessed that Nathan was one of those lonely souls who watched C-SPAN through the night—as though hauling contraband toilets had been his idea all along.

And if Nathan had asked why didn't they just sell toilets to Americans—that *was*, after all, legal if done in Canada, and, because of NAFTA, was even duty-free—Wayne would have to explain how things had become complicated between Gordie and him. When his father died Wayne assumed they would run the shop as equals, as partners, carrying on their father's name, eventually giving the business to their own sons. Gordie, older by eleven months and knowing the advantage that came with his tradesman's card, was quick to point out that only one of them was a plumber and furthermore, only the plumber among them was left the business in their father's will. Wayne took this all in stride, for the most part because everything they ever had, ever shared, as brothers had been mediated through a process of constant fighting, and he imagined that this would be no different than a baseball glove or who got to drive the truck on an after-hours call with their dad. This was different, though. Wayne was given a salary while the profits from the shop fell Gordie's way, and maybe that wasn't even Gordie's fault but his wife Lynne's, who seemed to lord it over Shirley and him whenever they got together. A couple of years into working at the business full-time, after the spats and silences began to build up between them, Wayne finally realized where he stood when Gordie hired Lynne's brother Derrick to computerize the inventory and modernize the shop. Derrick, who had just finished university and was in the habit of waving his business degree in people's faces as though it were a winning lottery ticket, spent more and more time at the shop, appropriating some office space in the back, poring over the books that Wayne kept and pointing out all the little accounting irregularities that would get them audited, that is, *if* Gordie believed they were honest mistakes. Wayne didn't have much of a choice from that point on.

Wayne was happy Nathan kept the personal questions to a minimum. It saved him from having to explain that he'd been asked to leave the shop after the accusations had been made, or describing the fight that ensued and how many OPP cars arrived to break it up, and how the only reason he wasn't arrested was because he played a year of Junior A hockey with one of the officers who showed up that night. He was glad Nathan didn't ask because it was difficult to admit that these events had left him with no toilets to sell and nowhere to sell them from. It wasn't as if they were hauling contraband cigarettes, he wasn't a common crook, he reasoned: he had a connection to toilets. There was history.

"Have you ever taken a toilet apart?" Wayne asks Nathan.

"Not deliberately," the young man replies.

"I was seven when I took my first one apart. A Crane, standard. It wasn't much of a job really. I remember I went with my dad on a call and while he was getting his gear up from the truck I had a look in the tank and could see that the problem was with the float arm; it wasn't fastened properly. And by the time he got up I had screwed the float arm support into position."

Nathan nods. The windshield grows tiny jewels of precipitation. Near the edges of the windshield, the drops bead into a stream that flutters near the edge and then is carried off.

"He gave me fifty dollars. It was like a million back then. He told me I did the work, so I got the pay."

They find an FM station that didn't brag about playing four songs in a row, and turn up the volume. Nathan lowers the window a crack and eases his fingers through the opening.

"How come you're not a plumber?"

"It takes a lot of time to become a plumber."

Wayne speaks the words reflexively, as he has done for so many years, all his life, but this time he hears the words, how quickly they come. How meaningless they are. Late one night after his insomnia and a snarl of twisted bed sheets had chased him from the bed, he turned on the television and watched one of those infomercials about personal improvement: the one where the guy with the smile full of Chiclets teeth sits on the yacht talking about how everything in your life—all the bad real estate decisions, the weight gain, the needle marks, (Christ, Wayne thought, feeling momentarily successful, needle marks *and* bad real estate investing: *that's* mass marketing)—could be traced back to one moment, one seemingly insignificant detail. He watched the sports highlights and the scrambled porn station until he became nauseated and then went back to bed and in the morning, he knew. He knew it as if that horse-faced man had personally visited him and placed the answer on his pillow like a fancy-hotel mint. He was in this situation because Gordie had bad ankles.

"They had me pegged for a pro career," Wayne says to Nathan, who only has to look back at Wayne to register his confusion. "I played Junior A. Shirley never told you?" Why should he be surprised? Shirley could be that way, her girlfriends would know about his personal embarrassments almost before he had time to concoct plausible alternate stories, but any point of pride was hidden away like a bridesmaid's dress after the reception. "I played Junior A, a year of it for the Spitfires."

"Oh yeah? Did you get drafted by a pro team?"

"No. I was scouted but I tore my ACL and medial collateral in the playoffs my first year. I couldn't come back."

"Did you play college?"

"No. Once you sign for a Junior A team, you lose eligibility."

That was it really. He was going to be the hockey player while his brother, the sullen ankle-skater, would be chosen to carry on the tradition for the family. No one had asked them of course; it was just the way things worked out. After he got hurt, he didn't get depressed like other guys who started drinking, and he didn't try to get some bullshit job on the fringes of the game like servicing Zambonis or selling skate sharpeners, he just stopped playing hockey and that was it. Maybe he had gotten enough out of hockey, he thought; he had met Shirley at a game against Oshawa and they married the summer after reconstructive surgery gave him a left knee that looked like a roadmap to Wawa. She helped him, she really did, and after a while he didn't want hockey, didn't look at the rink as they drove by or curse the cement heads in the pros who made millions for a couple of graceless goals a year.

After he and his brother stopped talking, his life had begun to take on the dimensions of failure, a feeling like he got in hotel rooms, of something smaller and emptier that somehow denied its own shabbiness. He saw less of his mother, who, although claiming neutrality, gravitated to the son who had carried on the family name in public. It was understandable. But now Wayne could not get to sleep; instead he took to nightly wanderings of the darkened house, ruminating on the turns of fortune that had stranded him. Shirley actually accused him of muttering, which he denied with a vehemence that even he recognized admitted guilt. His mood soured and the house became airless and small when they were both home. With Wayne out of work, she had taken on extra shifts at the day-care and found herself promoted after a few months to assistant manager. She had a knack with kids, and when he went to pick her up he would invariably find her with a child in her arms, some fear being calmed. They talked about starting a family but agreed that things were too unsettled now. Still, he would watch her from the car, study how she handled the kids in the backyard of the day care. For every child that needed to climb into her lap there was another who would just stand beside her, occasionally touching her, as though that were enough.

An OPP car appears in the mirror, having crept up on them liking a basking shark. Wayne watches it in the side-view, lifting his eyes from the road often enough that Nathan begins to consult his mirror.

"Don't look, Nathan." Wayne says, now training his gaze from the corners of his eyes, keeping his head facing the oncoming road. "They don't want to hassle a truck doing the speed limit. They're looking for speeders."

The truck had been Mike's and their partnership born at a table filled with draught glasses at the Legion Hall. He knew Mike from around town, a guy who liked the Leafs instead of the Red Wings and voiced his support without reservation. Wayne had witnessed the big man pick up and throw a rival fan into a dumpster and lean over the edge to shout into the filth and darkness that Gordie Howe was a faggot. When Mike wasn't frothing over dumpstered foes or visiting his probation officer, he loomed in the local sports bars like a very aggrieved beer commercial, patriotic and mountainously simple, expressing his incomprehension that any Canadian could root for an American team. So Wayne was petrified when Mike sat down beside him that night in the Legion Hall, thinking he had somehow incurred the big man's wrath, upset him with a look or a sleight against his beloved blue-and-white. It turned out that Mike was a fan of *his*; he knew Wayne from his days on the Spitfires and said he was sorry about the knee. He had potential, Mike said, emptying the remains of a pitcher into his and Wayne's glass. Mike knew everything about Wayne's career, even his statistics. He could describe the bodycheck in the game in which Wayne's future ended. He knew which knee had been torn up. They sat for hours talking about hockey, which they recognized was code for talking about life: their disappointments and aspirations, why they were underdogs, how they could turn their luck around. Wayne ordered another pitcher and told Mike about his brother and the problems at the shop. It was therapeutic—just having someone he didn't know sit there and listen—and Wayne found himself able to say things that he could never share with Shirley. Mike told him that he was looking for a partner for the short haul trips he was making, nothing perishable or requiring refrigeration, just transporting radios or electrical equipment. It was a job, and given Wayne's unemployment, it seemed like a godsend. They closed the place that Saturday, staggering out into the smell that Sarnia always has on cold October nights, and declared themselves partners.

Although it was Mike's truck, Wayne ended up doing most of the driving. It was an unspoken agreement and Wayne didn't mind it at all, though he would never tell Mike that. Complaint was their common language, grunted intermittently during their runs across southwestern Ontario and while Wayne feigned irritation at pulling the longer shifts, he found himself admitting that he was happy. The store became a distant memory and the altercations with his brother, just a hard time, a bad patch that he had put behind him.

It came as a shock when Mike announced that he was moving to Windsor to take a job at the new casino. He broke it to Wayne over a beer after a run to London, and was uncharacteristically sheepish about it, shifting in his seat as though he were trying to find a set of missing car keys. They were quiet on the trip home, which Mike interpreted as Wayne's anger but which was really Wayne trying to calculate the value of the truck and how much the monthly payments would set him back.

Nathan blows his nose and shoots a glance at the side-view mirror.

"They're gone."

"Yeah."

Nathan nods in acknowledgement. He is deep in thought, taking pains to fold the road map that has been spread open on his lap for the entire journey. He stops folding the map. It sits in his hands. Nathan looks puzzled, as though he were surprised that the paper folds into nothing more exotic than a rectangle.

In the distance Wayne sees the silhouette of Detroit's Renaissance Center framing the more modest skyline of Windsor. He thinks of all the porcelain they are hauling, and after that comes the inevitable calculations—two hundred big flush bowls at one hundred and fifty bucks per. After down-shifting, he feels the engagement of the metal, the shudder and hesitation. He senses the weight of his cargo pulling at him.

Shirley hadn't been pleased. While she had welcomed the money, she wondered why Wayne couldn't get something in town. Sarnia was starting to come back to life after the down times; there were jobs posted in the papers every day, she told him, but he was focused on the truck. He had spoken to someone at the bank about a loan, had the truck inspected and, as much as he trusted his friend, made sure their were no liens against the vehicle, before he sat down with Shirley and they added up the numbers on a piece of paper. The numbers: the earnest addition and calculation of margins, the canary-coloured paper that held it all like some receptacle of his desire. She looked at his calculations and, knowing what they meant to him, could not say no. And in the quiet early hours of the morning as he lay in bed, unable to sleep with the excitement and anxiety turning over in his stomach, he allowed himself the dream of seeing the truck not just as a means of earning a living but perhaps, the start of something bigger. As he drifted off again in the minutes before the alarm rang, he floated through scenes of his life, of what it had been and what he hoped it would become: he hovered through a garage where a fleet of new twelve-tons stood with his name emblazoned on their sides; in his brother's darkened shop he sat silently among the fixtures and equipment; from a stratospheric height he surveyed a landscape traversed by his trucks. Shirley had to shake him awake.

He bought the truck, and a world of complications appeared to him as clearly and immediately as if he had been fitted with a special set of glasses. Out of necessity, all considerations ultimately divided into revenues and expenditures, and the many other variables seemed reducible, subsidiary to a final tally. It was no longer possible to be indifferent because nothing in his life had that pleasing neutrality to it anymore; there was, at best, only the hope of a balance of gains and losses, a break-even proposition, and even this was provisional. It took its toll on him. Every pothole was personal, insulting him, eating away at his investment. He felt the tires wear and imagined a thin layer of his steel-belteds coating the asphalt of the province. He watched the price of diesel like it was a measure of the function of an ailing, solitary kidney. For the life of him, he couldn't find the profit margin like Mike could. He was an independent trucker now and he was going broke for his efforts.

He got the idea for the run after hearing about a home renovations kingpin in Ann Arbor whose store was allegedly selling the big flush. He still knew people in wholesaling, people who remembered his father and maybe didn't know that he was no longer working with Gordie, and buying two hundred units wouldn't arouse that much suspicion. He maxed out the credit card, canting *it takes money to make money* as the order was processed—but his hand shook as he signed the bill anyway. Getting the replacement boxes, the ones that were for six litre bowls and not the big flush units, proved to be surprisingly difficult, and it took weeks of cajoling general contractors for an odd, discarded box before it occurred to Wayne that he could make a preliminary trip to Ann Arbor and maybe cut a deal that would provide him with all the counterfeit packaging that he needed to conceal his cargo.

That first trip, several weeks before he had planned the big flush run, brought him face to face with Stan Stepzcincski, the self-proclaimed czar of Midwest home renovations. The renovation business had taken off and Stan the Man had been there with his big-box store ready to accommodate all the home-supply needs of eastern and central Michigan. Old Ann Arbor homesteads were being gutted and redone by young professionals, flipped for double their purchase price. New mansions, comparable with anything in Auburn Hills or Grosse Pointe, were sprouting like beautiful cabbages, *and who didn't want to make their own home a little more …livable?* asked the Czar, offering Wayne a coffee in his office that looked out over two hundred thousand square feet of retail space. Wayne thought that he would conduct his business with the manager of the plumbing department, but once he told the manager of his proposal, he was ushered up to meet the great man himself. Wayne tried to contain his excitement as he was escorted through the fluorescent-lit universe of hardware; it was clear that the demand for the big flush units was insatiable, and that any deal would be a big one requiring the Czar's personal approval. Wayne was surprised to find the Czar a small man, five-six, maybe five-seven, the type who in another ten years would be called spry. He had blue eyes and a crew cut and was friendly but serious in that sleeves-up, self-made-man sort of way. The Czar told him his life story, the flight from Szczecin in the thirties, Lady Liberty and the cold stone face of Ellis Island, hard times growing up in Hamtramck. He had organized festivities for the Pope's visit in the eighties, owned a luxury box at Tiger's Stadium and now endowed a Chair in Architecture at the University.

The Czar leaned back in his chair and smiled. Was that the

point of the audience? Wayne waited for the hard bargaining to begin. He looked around for the plumbing supplies manager, imagining that someone must be laughing their asses off at the sight of this audience, but he and the Czar were alone in the room. Wayne smiled but tried not to smile too much. *Americans.* Everyone a hero. As the Czar went on to rhapsodize about the big flush units, Wayne could imagine a single instrument rising in accompaniment behind him. A bugle or a banjo.

"These aren't just toilets, you know," the Czar said, pulling Wayne close with a voice that was soft and hard at the same time, as though through the grilles of a confessional. "They're symbols. They hearken back to an earlier time, a sanctity of the home, a freedom of choice that's all but gone. Wayne, people want to hear that water, that *Niagara*." The Czar made a fist with both hands and shook them as he mouthed the word *Niagara* again.

By day's end Wayne was headed back for the border with two hundred empty six-litre boxes crammed into and strapped on the roof of Shirley's Honda, along with a handshake agreement— which, coming from the Czar, was assuredly as credible as a baptismal certificate signed by the holy father himself—that he would return with the treasure that they so dearly sought.

Nathan has dozed off but rouses as Wayne brings the truck to a stop on Aylmer Street. With the velocity and diversions of the open road gone, Wayne fidgets with excess energy. He smacks out the drum intro to "Long, Lonely Time" on the steering wheel. He turns up the radio, letting the splashing high-hat and the wailing awaken Nathan further. The clouds ahead of them, which have all morning been arranging themselves into a black mantle obscuring the sun and sheeting rain, have thinned into a modest, milky film, spread evenly against the mid-afternoon sky. In the distance Wayne can make out the slope and arch of the Ambassador Bridge. The U.S. Immigration and Customs house sat at the near end of the bridge, a homey single-storey building made to look like a school-house or town hall from which an armed man in a trooper hat and mirror shades would sidle out to ask him, with that implacable trooper calm, *What do you have to declare?* It has become hot and Wayne finds himself breathing heavily, mildly uncomfortable in his seat. He opens his window wide and loosens the shoulder strap of his seat belt but nothing eases his discomfort, and now Nathan is noticing.

"You okay?" he asks.

"Oh, yeah," Wayne says. He senses his heart racing and hears a noise inside his head like a siren in the distance, approaching.

"You're grey, man. Do you want to get out?" Nathan says, turning off the radio as if for emphasis.

"No. I'm okay."

The light changes and they pull off Aylmer and onto University Street. Wayne reasons that his discomfort will pass but it doesn't; now he is hungry for air, for any type of relief, and pulls the truck off the road into the first available parking lot, where he fishes out ten bucks and throws it at the attendant. It is another five minutes before he can catch his breath, hunched over the front wheel-well, dripping sweat and sucking oxygen like he did when he was double-shifted an entire game.

"Chest pain?" Nathan asks, bending over to try and see Wayne's face. "Any pain in the throat or into the arm?"

"No," Wayne says, "I think I've just got the flu or something."

"Do you want me to call Shirley?"

Wayne straightens. Just the motion of becoming vertical makes the world seem to inhale and exhale around him. The edges of his vision ripple and he tries not to pitch backwards. It is dusk and noon within seconds.

"No. Let's not worry her."

"Are you taking some sort of stimulant Wayne?" says Nathan, bending forward and speaking in a hushed voice.

"No."

"Between you and me, Wayne."

"No. And fuck off."

Nathan lifts his hands and shakes his head in exasperation. He gets out of the truck. Nathan is walking away now, determinedly, as though for a bus station or a new life, and it takes all the energy that Wayne has to catch up with him and apologize.

"Save it." Nathan says, continuing down the sidewalk. "Come on, we're almost there."

"It's bad enough you treat me like some sort of retard, but, you know, it's not like I'm responsible for any of this."

"For any of what?"

Nathan stops. He looks at Wayne and pauses.

"I heard you're going to lose your truck."

"Who told you that? Did Shirley tell you that?"

Nathan takes a step backward, sensing a field fully mined.

"No. She didn't say anything."

"What did she say?"

"Nothing. Look, it's just that you pay me at the end of the day, you know? Nothing up front, low overhead, and what we're hauling…"

"What about it?"

"Nothing, I just don't like being lied to."

"It's fucking toilets for Christ sake."

"I want a cut."

"You—" Wayne's smile is twisted, the indignation of Shirley's betrayal and Nathan's effrontery invigorating him, "you want a *cut*?"

Nathan sports a pallor now, but he stands his ground.

"Yeah. I want a cut. If something happens, I'll have to answer for it as well. I want a cut."

"How much of a cut do you think you deserve?" says Wayne, walking up to the younger man in such a way that is designed to make the lesser of the two parties cower. He has seen all forms of bravado on the ice, how the game is not turned on shots or saves but on glances cast and seething oaths. In this world, a guy like Nathan would be a goalie, a masked man in a protective shell, full of tics and rituals, shuffling in his crease, waiting to be beaten.

"Five percent."

"Three percent and we have a deal."

"Okay."

He shoots, he scores. Five-hole.

Wayne juts out his chin in the direction of a restaurant across the street. A conciliatory move, something to vent the steam after their haggling. Nathan nods and crosses the road with him. Inside the restaurant—a fast-food place fronted by a kids play-structure of plastic tubes and pipes that reminds him of Sarnia—he buys Nathan a burger and some fries and they sit down in a molded plastic booth. He feels sorry for the kid, wants to foster a new spirit of partnership. He'd like him to dig in, but Nathan hovers over his meal. It occurs to Wayne that Shirley must have told her entire family about their money troubles for it to have filtered down to Nathan. He is surprised at how calm he is, he thought he would have felt more aggrieved but after a moment of anger it has washed over him and now that everything is out in the open he feels oddly magnanimous. He goes over the numbers again: two hundred units at one-hundred *American* in profit per unit, with seven hundred, maybe seven fifty to Nathan—without the kid knowing the net he could have offered him twenty percent, fifty, even, yeah, *even-Steven*. He should have asked that Nathan pay half the fuel costs.

"Do you want to go to the casino?" Wayne says, leaving a tip half hidden under his plate.

"Are you kidding?"

"We're ahead of schedule. I got nothing to do except deliver toilets and I got a friend who works there who I'd like to touch base with."

"Yeah, well. If we're close."

It's only four blocks to the casino, a renovated mall with an atrium grafted onto the open sore of its face. A fountain gurgles up a frothy spume that draws stares from a busload of seniors ready to disembark. At seeing the entrance, done up in high seventies style with a costumed doorman doffing his hat at patrons, Wayne for a moment considers that he and Nathan may be underdressed. He expects the strictly enforced glamour of a scene from a Bond movie, summer tuxedoes, watches that cost more than his truck. But once inside the violently air-conditioned central hall he is surprised to see that a form of gaming democracy has been established, with all denominations, including his, enthusiastically welcomed. Nathan looks shell-shocked, unnerved by the non-stop barrage of bells and sirens, an onslaught loud enough for Wayne to suspect it could be used as a form of torture or a cure for autism, something the casino's management has no doubt put in place to heighten the gaming excitement.

"I'll meet you back here in a half-hour." Wayne shouts at Nathan. He hands the younger man something. Nathan finds a twenty in his hand. "An advance on three percent."

Nathan nods and Wayne has disappeared into the shifting crowd. A buzzer is set off, rising above the general din, and balloons are released from the ceiling. Someone has won a jackpot. Nathan searches for a cashier to buy some chips.

Wayne walks through the main floor of the casino, looking for Mike. He imagines that Mike would be a pit boss, although he isn't quite sure what that job entails, but thinks it is probably like a foreman for all the employees in a certain sector of the casino. Wayne will be the first to admit that he isn't a gambler himself, cannot even bring himself to buy a lottery ticket, and the crowd around the blackjack tables and roulette wheels does not inspire him to change his ways. He imagined it would be like the commercials on television, happy people relaxing and enjoying themselves, but the faces he sees are like those of people struggling through a day of desk work, counting twenties in a bank somewhere or filling out forms to order more forms. A hypnotic look prevails, penned veal or toll-booth attendant eyes, as though not trying to attract attention from the closed-circuit camera that aims to capture their every card-counting gesture. Mike is nowhere to be found, probably on another shift, he thinks. After a quick tour of the craps tables, Wayne finds a security guard standing by a bank of slot machines.

"Do you know if Mike Babson is working tonight?"

"We got four hundred people working here, sir, I don't know most their names."

"Tall guy, red hair."

"I couldn't tell you even if I knew the guy. Casino policy."

The security guard turns away and Wayne takes a long look around but he has given up on finding anyone familiar. The room seems big and empty, a place near closing, but the noise grows, out of the empty space it builds and echoes until it sounds to Wayne like the static of a poorly tuned radio. Near the entrance he finds Nathan waiting for him. He has taken his chips and, lacking the nerve to gamble, cashed them back in for his twenty dollars.

"I got the same bill back," he explains, giddy, a complimentary drink in his hand, "I memorized the serial number. What are the odds of that happening?"

"Long, I suppose."

Outside, the air is wet with smells from the Detroit River. Nathan pockets the twenty and walks on, slightly ahead of Wayne. His arms, thin but well-muscled, swing loosely at his side as he ambles up the sidewalk to the lot where they are parked. He reminds Wayne of Shirley, the small frame common to all the Gibson clan, even the men, apparently.

"Did you find your friend?"

"No. He wasn't working today."

Wayne starts the truck and pulls it onto University Street, following the signs that lead to Huron Church Road and the bridge. The truck comes to a stop at the foot of the Ambassador. It is past three o'clock now, and traffic is backed up from the Immigration and Customs office. They pull forward in fits of foot-pounds of torque and sour diesel smoke, advancing in car-length increments along the upslope of the superstructure. Now they are above

Windsor, and Wayne looks down to see the casino in the city centre, crumpled like a wounded animal, as though it had fallen between existing banks of office towers. The sun is out, flooding the cab and drawing shadows under every car. It is at that moment that Wayne feels the desire to turn back, to get the truck out of its lane and ride down the incline back to Windsor. It is not like before, this feeling, and his heart beats calmly, as though fear has been cordoned off in another part of his body. He thinks of a word to describe it but he is at a loss for such words. It almost feels as though he is on the ice again, watching the world of possibilities tumble around him, knowing that he can enter this world and take what he wants from it. But it is not this because there is a sadness to it, an ache, something he has never felt in a hockey game. By the time they are near the u.s customs house, he knows that it is a different type of longing, and again he feels the need to throw the truck into reverse. The truck, however, is hemmed into a line that can proceed only in one direction, and maneuvering the vehicle out of its lane and across the median is plainly impossible. But he feels such an ache, for a moment imagining Shirley cradling someone else's child, wondering if she is thinking of him at all, of where he is. He wants the feeling to pass but knows it will not. It is an appetite for something he has not yet tasted and all he is certain of is that the hunger can only grow. He can feel the cargo behind him, pulling and shifting, porcelain grinding like a mouth full of molars. The truck full of toilets slouches forward another twenty feet. They're at the customs house now. People search for their passports and cargo manifests. America lies ahead, a huge, waking dream waiting to be entered into.

LIAM DURCAN

ESPLANADE
Books

THE FICTION SERIES AT VÉHICULE PRESS

[Series Editor: Andrew Steinmetz]

A House by the Sea
A novel by Sikeena Karmali

A Short Journey by Car
Stories by Liam Durcan

Seventeen Tomatoes: Tales from Kashmir
Stories by Jaspreet Singh

Véhicule Press
www.vehiculepress.com